A BREATH
of
FRESH
AIR

A BREATH
of
FRESH
AIR

AMULYA MALLADI

BALLANTINE BOOKS
NEW YORK

A Ballantine Book
Published by The Ballantine Publishing Group

Copyright © 2002 by Amulya Malladi

www.ballantinebooks.com

Library of Congress Cataloging-in-Publication Data
can be obtained from the publisher upon request.

ISBN 0-345-45028-0

Text design by Holly Johnson

Manufactured in the United States of America

First Edition: July 2002

10   9   8   7   6   5   4   3   2   1

For Søren

ACKNOWLEDGMENTS

I will always be indebted to my amazing agent, Milly Marmur, who had more faith and patience than I. My sincere thanks to Anika Streitfeld for her insight and to Amandeep Singh and Jody Pryor for their unstinting support. I can't thank Mamta Puri enough for her help in writing this book and Dhruv Puri for letting his mother speak with me on the telephone for hours. My thanks also to Arjun for his unswerving friendship and encouragement.

PROLOGUE

ANJALI

DECEMBER 3, 1984
BHOPAL RAILWAY STATION
BHOPAL, INDIA

I waited patiently for the first hour, and then I started to get impatient. The Bhopal Railway Station was abuzz with late-night activities. The homeless were wandering, begging for money and food; some people were waiting for their train to arrive and others, like me, were waiting for someone to pick them up, as the hands of the big dirty clock in front of me came together to welcome midnight.

I turned my wrist again to look at the watch my husband had given me after our wedding just a few months ago. It was a nice Titan watch, with a green background and red numbers and hands. It was a compulsive action to look at the watch, since I already knew what the time was.

Why wasn't he here? He knew when I was getting back. He had bought the tickets himself. How could he have forgotten?

Soon the homeless stopped begging and started looking for places to settle in for the night. The Station Master used a long, thick wooden stick to prod the homeless, who were sleeping in front of his office and the waiting rooms, into moving. He was successful with some and unsuccessful with others. He looked at me curiously and then ignored me. He had probably seen many women wait for their husbands or loved ones at the railway station.

I flipped once again through the *Femina* magazine I had bought at the Hyderabad Railway Station. By now I had read all the articles and the short story, and the advertisements, but I looked through them once more to avoid staring at the dirty white clock or my beautiful watch.

"*Memsaab*, taxi?" a Sardarji taxi driver asked me.

I inched farther back into the metal chair I was sitting on, grasping my purse tightly in my lap and moving my sari-clad leg to touch my small suitcase in a subconscious effort to protect it.

"No," I said, and focused on the slightly crumpled pages of my magazine.

"Late in the night it is now, *Memsaab*." Sardarji was undeterred by my casual refusal. "Not safe it is at the station."

I let the fear of being accosted late in the night pass first. My husband would be here soon, I told myself. I thought up an excuse: His scooter must have broken down. I thought up another: The tire must have been punctured. It happened all the time on the bad roads of Bhopal.

"Where do you have to go?" Sardarji asked me.

I took a deep breath and looked at him. He didn't look dangerous in the dim yellow lights of the railway station, but you can never tell by someone's face what he is capable of.

"Bairagarh," I said succinctly, and he moved away from

me without comment. The EME Center was in Bairagarh and if I lived there, I was an army wife, and he probably didn't want to mess with me.

I kept time with my shifting feet and the rustle of the oft-turned pages of the magazine, pages that didn't look brand-new and glossy anymore, but were wrinkled like the ones roadside peanut vendors wrapped fried peanuts in. My eyes wandered to the entrance of the station, again and again looking for a familiar face.

I didn't even know how to get in touch with my husband—we didn't have a phone. Colonel Shukla did. I could call him, I thought, and then decided against it. How would it look if people knew my husband forgot to pick me up?

I turned my head when there was a small commotion at the other end of the station, and it started then. Slowly, but surely, it spread.

I became aware of it for the first time when I inhaled and felt my lungs being scratched by nails from the inside, like someone had thrown red chili powder into my nose. I took another breath and it didn't change. I clasped my throat and closed my eyes as they started to burn and water. Something was wrong, my mind screamed wildly as I, along with the others, tried to seek a reason for the tainted air we were breathing.

Sardarji, who was standing nearby, looked at me, our eyes matching the panic that was spreading through the railway station. The homeless had started gathering their meager belongings, while others were standing up, moving, looking around, asking questions, trying to find out what could be done. Soon it became unbearable and the exodus began. People started to clamor to get out of the station. The entrance was jam-packed;

3

heaving bodies slammed against each other as they tried to squeeze past the small entrance to save their lives. Some people jumped across the tracks to get to the other platform and look for an exit from there. People were everywhere, like scrounging ants looking for food.

"Taxi, *Memsaab,*" Sardarji cried out as he came toward me.

I didn't question his generosity and picked up my suitcase and started to run along with him to the entrance. Our bodies joined the others as we looked for a small hole, a pathway, out of the railway station. People were running helter-skelter, trying to breathe. Something is wrong, I thought again, this time in complete panic, something about the air in the railway station is very wrong.

The struggle to get out of the station became harder because no one could breathe. My lungs felt like they would implode and even though I tried to suck in as much air as I could, it was not really air that I was breathing. It was something toxic, something acrid, something that was burning my insides and scratching my eyes. Each breath I took made me dizzy and the burning sensation, that terrible burning sensation, wouldn't go away.

My suitcase and purse got lost somewhere in the crowd, but I was half-crazed with the need to breathe and forgot about them.

Sardarji was having trouble breathing as well. His voice was high-pitched and shaky and I could hear him hiss as he tried to breathe. He pointed in the direction of his taxi and we started running, pushing past people who just like us were trying to find a way out. It looked like every automobile in the city was out on the streets. The sound of honking vehicles mingled with the cries for help, while the city stood bright, lit up with car, scooter, and auto rickshaw headlights, like a bride covered in gold and diamonds just before her wedding.

"What's happening?" someone screamed.

"Run, out of the city, out of the city!" someone else cried out.

We reached the taxi and as soon as we got inside, people clamored and banged at the car windows.

For once, compassion failed me. "Drive," I said through my misery, and the engine mercifully started.

Navigating the taxi out of the crowded parking lot, where cars lay haphazardly like dead and wounded soldiers in a battle-field, proved to be difficult. Sardarji tried his best. The honking of his taxi joined the sounds of other impatient cars. It was get-ting increasingly difficult to drive. The crowds were blocking the way and our inability to breathe was not helping either.

I held the edge of my sari to my nose, hoping to dissipate some of the spice in the air, but nothing would make the air clean.

A few cars moved and we managed to get to the road, which could just as well have been a parking lot itself because the cars were not moving. As I struggled to stay alive, a new fear gripped me. Was my husband caught in this? I shuddered at the thought and prayed he had indeed forgotten to pick me up. But if he had come and picked me up when my train ar-rived two hours ago, we would have been safe. I would have been safe, my mind cried out.

"*Memsaab*, we will never get out of here," Sardarji said, stumbling over the words. "Maybe we should get out of the car and run."

"Run where?" I asked, hysteria sprinkled over my voice. "Where would we go?"

When he didn't answer, I turned to him and saw him lying on the steering wheel. I shook him hard, screaming for him to wake up and drive us out of there.

He managed to straighten himself, but before he could step on the accelerator or drive into the space the car ahead of us had made, he collapsed on the steering wheel again, and this time I couldn't wake him up.

My heart felt like it had stopped beating for an instant. I didn't know how to drive; I had never learned. My husband and I didn't even have a car. I wanted to help Sardarji, check on him, but I couldn't, I couldn't even breathe, and suddenly nothing seemed more important than breathing. I had taken it for granted all my life and now I couldn't breathe without feeling my insides rip open against the onslaught of the spice in the air.

I opened the taxi door and pushed into the people who swarmed around the car. There was no relief for anyone.

Someone got into the taxi as soon as I left and I saw Sardarji's lifeless body being pushed out of the driver's seat onto the road.

I looked around as people jostled me, searching for a way out. People were running in all directions and I wondered, Which one was the right direction? Which direction gave you life? I moved aimlessly, going first in one direction and then in another. The world revolved around me in slow motion as my eyes started to shut on their own accord. I knew that I was going to join Sardarji.

It was then, when I was almost sure that I was going to

die, that I saw an army Jeep, and it looked like a beacon of hope. I cried out for help, but my voice was drowned by the voices of others, screaming and yelling and demanding the gods for an answer.

I think the Jeep driver saw me first, and then someone from inside called out to me. They knew my name and they knew whose wife I was. I felt relief sweep through me, even as energy seeped out. Just like it happens in the movies, I quietly collapsed onto the asphalt road.

My eyes had trouble adjusting to the whiteness. Everything around me was white. But I knew I was not dead. I knew I was in a hospital because of the telltale smell of medicines. I lifted my hands but couldn't see anything. I could feel there were tubes going into my nose and some were coming out of my hands. I felt like an octopus.

I wanted to talk, to ask someone what was going on, but my throat was clogged, and then I remembered in fuzzy detail the night I thought I had died. I breathed in with trepidation and was relieved to not feel any burning, but my lungs still felt full and heavy, as if water had been pumped into them.

I licked my dry lips and tried to speak. I called out for my husband and waited, but I wasn't sure if I was making enough sound to attract his attention. I wasn't even sure if anyone was near me. I could hear some voices at a distance, far away.

I could not concentrate clearly on anything, but I heard the faint voice of a newscaster saying something about a Union Carbide factory and some gas that had leaked into the city of Bhopal.

❧ O N E

A N J A L I

SEPTEMBER 2000

OOTY, INDIA

The fog was rolling softly into the vegetable bazaar and people were flocking around the vendors in woolen shawls and sweaters. The smell of burning coal and corn permeated the market from the stall where fresh corn was being roasted on hot coals. A few people were gathered around the corn stall, warming their hands by the coal, waiting for their corn to be ready.

It was like any other evening. The day was coming to an end and people were getting ready for dinner, bargaining with the shopkeepers, choosing the right vegetables for their meal.

The bitter gourd was just ripe enough and I brought it close to my nose. My weathered Pashmina shawl was slipping from my shoulders so I pulled it up. That was when I saw him, from the corner of my eye, my nose still taking in the scent of the gourd. It took a moment to register who he was—for an instant he was just a familiar face. His eyes lifted and he saw me. I let the shawl fall.

I wanted to pretend I didn't see him. It would be easier to do that, but cowardly, and I hadn't lived through thirty-seven cycles of this earth for nothing. I straightened my back as if I could feel him stare at me and I was tempted to turn around hastily to see if he was. But I didn't want to do that. What if he wasn't looking at me? What if he didn't recognize me at all?

"Two kilos," I murmured, half-dazed, to the vegetable vendor. He instantly lifted his metal scale and let it hang from his hand. Usually I paid attention so I didn't end up paying more for less goods, but this time my heart was beating a little too fast for the small details to matter. The vendor put a two-kilo weight on one of the weighing plates and started piling the gourds on the other. I held up my cloth bag and he poured the gourds inside.

After paying for them, I turned around, boldly lifting my eyes, surveying the evening vegetable market as if I were looking for the next thing I needed for dinner.

He was gone and I was disappointed.

I bought some tomatoes and onions. My mind was blank and suddenly I doubted what I had seen. Had he really been there? Or did I mistake someone else for him?

It had to be him, I thought defensively, as I paid another vendor twenty *rupees* for half a kilo of tomatoes. It was September and tomatoes were not in season. If it was July, I would have paid less than half.

"Anju . . . Anjali?" a vaguely familiar, slightly unsure voice called from behind and I felt relief swarm through me. He recognized me; he wasn't ignoring me.

I turned around as if unaware of who it was. I had practiced this in my head numerous times in past years. He would say hello and my eyes would glaze over. I would nod my head and ask him if I was supposed to know him. He would say his name and I would let my eyes brighten with recognition. Somehow, I had always hoped I would not recognize him.

But fantasies are easy to conjure, while reality is unchangeable. I smiled at him. I couldn't ask him if I was supposed to know him—that would be juvenile.

"Yes," I managed to say.

"Anju," he repeated. "It's me, Prakash."

I didn't need him to tell me his name, I thought angrily. I wouldn't forget him. I couldn't forget him.

"Prakash," I said, and cleared my throat unnecessarily. "What are you doing here?"

"I'm posted in Wellington," he said, his eyes still filled with disbelief.

The Defense Services Staff College was in Wellington, Ooty, and it shouldn't have surprised me that he was posted here. But I was surprised, maybe because in my imagination I had always thought I'd meet him when I was looking like a knockout and my hair was in place in a sophisticated knot. But my hair was not in place, my braid was limp, and strands of dry hair were stubbornly pushing out of the folds I had made in the morning. It had been months since I had dyed my hair, so the white streaks were everywhere. My sari was cotton and lime green and wrinkled, and my blood red shawl clashed with the green. No, I didn't look like a knockout. I looked like a weary woman at the end of a very long day.

"How long have you been here?" I asked politely.

"A month," he said. "And you?"

"Oh, I moved to Ooty a few years after . . ." I let my words trail away; he knew what I was talking about.

We stood in silence for about half a minute, when I said, "I should go, I have had a long day at work and . . ."

"So . . . you . . . you work?" he asked. "Are you married?"

"I am a teacher at the Ootacamund School and, yes . . . married," I said.

He nodded in response and then I nodded and then we nodded together, avoiding eye contact. We really didn't have anything to say to each other. All the speeches I had planned and everything I had intended to say were somehow lost in the reality of the situation and the shock of seeing his face again.

He was in mid-nod when a woman called out to him. He turned automatically and I took a step back.

"I need your purse," the woman said.

She was wearing an impeccable brown silk sari with a long flesh-colored woolen coat. She looked at me and smiled.

Prakash cleared his throat. "Ah, this is my wife Indira . . . Indu, and this is . . . ah . . . ah . . ."

I folded my hands and smiled as my adrenaline surged because of the unexpected shock. He had a wife!

"*Namaste,* I am Mrs. Sharma," I said, putting him out of his predicament.

"*Namaste,*" his wife said, trying to figure out how her husband would know me. She looked at Prakash quizzically and he blurted a few disjointed words, saying nothing, confusing everything.

"I knew Prakash a long time ago," I said easily, enjoying his discomfort.

"Ah," his wife said, and we all stood together in uncomfortable silence.

Unable to stand it any longer, I made my excuses by saying, "I should be going," before hurrying away.

I smiled maliciously when I heard his wife's sharp voice ask, "What does she mean by a long time ago?"

I walked home briskly, oblivious to my surroundings, to everything except the shock that was still simmering through my blood. Usually Sandeep, my husband, bought vegetables on his scooter, but today he was giving some of his students private tutoring.

I had always known that sometime, somewhere, I would meet Prakash again. I just hadn't thought it would be such an anticlimax. I had thought he would be apologetic and guilty for his actions. I had hoped he would be contrite, would apologize right off the bat, and I would wave his apology away. I couldn't forgive what he had done and it didn't seem relevant anymore either. It didn't matter whether he was sorry or not, it was over and done with and we had both moved on. I definitely had, because besides the shock of seeing him, I felt nothing. A mild confusion was traipsing through my brain but there was no bitterness left. Time made apologies and absolution unnecessary. Time didn't really heal, it just made bad memories distant so that the brain couldn't recapture the lost pain.

When I got home, my sister-in-law was waiting for me by the door, with a scowl on her face.

Komal had been living with us ever since her husband

died five years ago. Sandeep had told me she had no place to go and didn't ask for my permission before he invited her to stay with us. He had consulted with me, but what I had to say was immaterial. Komal *really* had no place to go.

We didn't get along. Our personalities were different and she never forgave me for marrying her brother. But she probably would have had the same problem regardless of which woman Sandeep married. Despite how our relationship was, I couldn't turn her out of my home and onto the streets. But disliking a sister-in-law and living with her are two completely different things. Komal knew that she was living in my house on sufferance, but that didn't stop her from trying to treat me like a daughter-in-law living in her husband's family home.

"You should have been home an hour earlier," she bellowed, as soon as I took my Kohlapuri slippers off on the wide veranda. I silently walked into the house and she followed me to the kitchen. I started to pull out the vegetables from the cloth bag and line them up next to the sink.

"Do you think I am the maid in this house?" she demanded.

I didn't respond. I had learned early on that Komal had a knack for asking rhetorical questions.

"I had to clean up after your son today. He dropped a glass of milk on the floor," she continued. Amar was not adept at holding heavy things; his fingers sometimes failed him, just like his legs did, and mishaps happened.

I shucked my shawl off and threw it from the kitchen into the living room, not caring where it fell. I could hear her speak even as I peeked inside Amar's room and found him sleeping contentedly. I would have to wake him up for dinner, I thought uneasily. I didn't like to wake him up. While he was asleep, he couldn't be sick. But he had to eat, even if it meant he had to face the world.

Komal was still complaining when I got back to the kitchen.

Didn't she see that I was trying to ignore her?

I started rinsing the vegetables and Komal raised her voice to be heard over the running water. It was bad enough that I had to cook dinner after a long day in school; it was worse that she clawed at me as soon as I got home.

"And why don't you come home early so that you can take care of Amar? Why do I have to do it all the time?"

Actually, Komal didn't have to take care of Amar. Sandeep and I had hired an ayah to take care of him after we moved to Ooty and I had started working. Once Komal moved in with us she said she wanted the job because she didn't have anything to do all day. Even though I resented having to rely on Komal, I was the first to admit that not hiring an ayah did save us money, something we always needed to do.

I maintained my silence and pulled out the wooden cutting board and knife.

"What, you have taken a *moun vrat* or something?"

I shook my head. No, I hadn't taken a vow of silence; I was just too tired to argue with her over something that didn't need to be argued over.

"These *karela* look bad," she commented on the bitter gourds I had just purchased. "Can't you go to the market to buy vegetables? It is just a kilometer away. Do you have to go to that cheap supermarket?"

I took a deep breath and, knife in hand, turned around to face her. "I did go to the market and there is nothing wrong with the supermarket, it is close by and it is cheap. Now if you don't leave me alone there will be no dinner before Sandeep gets home."

Komal knew that tone of voice, but it didn't mean she listened to it. She glared at me and then sniffed, bringing the edge of her sari to her face. She wiped her cheeks as if there were tears on them and sniffed some more.

"You talk like this to me because I don't have a husband."

I was in no mood for her emotional dramas. I just wanted to cook dinner and find a place in the house where I could put my feet up and calm down.

I peeled the coarse green skin of the bitter gourds and rubbed turmeric and salt on the white soft skin that lay beneath.

"You're making stuffed *karela*?" Komal demanded.

No, I was making potato curry! Heavens, couldn't the woman shut up for just a little while? Did she have to talk all the time? I understood that she was home alone all day and needed to pounce on me as soon as I got home, but understanding only went so far. She was tired of being locked up with Amar all day and I knew she needed the adult contact, but I had been locked up with students and teachers all day, and I needed the silence.

"I don't like *karela*," she complained. "Why do you make it when I don't like it?"

"Because they are in season," I said, as I made incisions in all the other gourds to put the stuffing in. "And I feel like stuffed *karela.*"

"Oh, we have to do everything the Queen feels like doing," she carped, and I wanted to throw the sharp knife at her. Thankfully I heard the front door open. Sandeep was finally home and Komal would go nag him for a while.

As soon as Sandeep stepped through the doorway, Komal rushed out of the kitchen. I heard her tell him about the stuffed bitter gourd curry I was making and how she didn't like it at all.

Sandeep spoke to her in a low voice. Sandeep always spoke in a low voice, as if what he was saying was so important that one had to pay all the attention one could to hear everything. That was one of the reasons why I had wanted to marry him. He was the calmest person I knew and I hoped it would rub off on me from time to time.

I abandoned the gourds on the counter and filled a steel bowl with water for Sandeep's tea. I put the water on the stove and added a spoonful of tea leaves and of sugar along with some milk to it. By the time Sandeep checked on Amar and came to the kitchen, I was pouring hot tea through a sieve into a cup.

"How was the tutoring class?" I asked, wanting the comfort of aimless conversation.

"These rich people's children can be very stupid," he said wearily, and sat down on the wooden chair I kept in the kitchen for him.

It was our daily ritual—Sandeep sat and talked to me while I cooked, and he helped with the dishes when I was done. Komal always objected to allowing the man of the house to soil his hands cleaning pots and pans, but Sandeep and I both ignored her. This was our home; we decided how we lived, and Sandeep was definitely not the average Indian male who thought helping his wife in the kitchen was below his dignity.

"Has Amar been sleeping long?" Sandeep asked as he stretched on the chair, sipping his tea.

"I don't know, I just got back. But he seems peaceful," I said, as I chopped a raw mango for the stuffing. I added a spoonful of turmeric, another spoonful of chili powder, a dash of fenugreek seeds, and some oil to the raw mangoes and mixed them together with my hand. I opened the gourds carefully to put the stuffing inside.

"Is Komal still at home?" I asked, because I couldn't hear the television in the drawing room. Komal always turned on the television, which she called her "only true companion."

"She left for Mala's house," Sandeep said.

Mala was our neighbor. Her husband was a salesman and he often went out of town. Komal spent most of her evenings and Sundays with Mala when Mala's husband was away. It was how it worked. Widows and housewives gossiped to pass the time: one to forget she didn't have a husband and the other to remember she had one even though he was hardly around.

"Komal's giving you a hard time, isn't she?"

I shook my head. I didn't want him to feel guilty for being a good older brother.

"It's just a bad day." I liberally poured peanut oil on a flat cooking pan, which used to be nonstick a long time ago.

"Something happened at school?" Sandeep asked.

I didn't know what to say, or even if I should say anything.

I didn't like having secrets from Sandeep. He was my husband, but that was a secondary title. He was my friend first. When the oil sizzled, I carefully added three gourds, one after the other, to the frying pan, all the while knowing that Sandeep was waiting for a response. He was attuned to me; he knew something was wrong and I did owe him an explanation.

"I met Prakash today."

The words clashed with the air around us with the same sizzle as the gourds when they were added to the hot oil. I had to jerk my hand away as the oil splattered a little.

It was not enough of an explanation. One didn't say something like that without something else bolstering it. It was like serving plain rice without curry for dinner.

I still couldn't face Sandeep; I didn't want to see what he was thinking. Sandeep had never told me how he felt about Prakash, even though I asked him numerous times. I told him what had happened in Bhopal, in my previous marriage, and he had listened sympathetically, but he hadn't passed judgment on Prakash. That was another thing I loved about Sandeep; he never came to a conclusion without knowing *all* the facts. He only knew my side of the story, he told me, and even though he was sorry about what happened, he couldn't think of Prakash as the villain. I remember him telling me that after what I had been through, I had to have the desire to blame someone. He understood that and hoped I would not give in to it. Sometimes life just took painful, unexpected turns and mortals had to accept them.

"He is posted to the Defense Staff College at Wellington," I added, as I rolled the gourds in the frying pan with a metal spatula. "I met him at the market . . . with his wife."

18

I didn't hear Sandeep move, so I was surprised when I felt his hand on my shoulder. He turned me around to look into my eyes. I escaped his gaze, staring at the rim of his brown plastic glasses.

"Is something wrong?" he asked calmly, as if I owed my turbulent emotions to more than seeing Prakash.

"I don't know," I said honestly.

He smiled and kissed me on the forehead. I think he was about to say something more but there was a noise from our son's room. Sandeep touched my cheek and left to check on Amar.

I washed some rice and put it along with some water into the small pressure cooker. I put the cooker on the gas stove and brought out yesterday's *dal* from the fridge. I heated it on midflame on the stove and tried to make sense of what I was feeling.

Sandeep had asked if something was wrong, and something was. I just didn't know what. It could be several things, I decided. I could be disturbed because Prakash was married, or that he didn't want to introduce me to his wife, or that Sandeep didn't seem to be shaken at all by my news.

There were times when I wished I could say or do something that would rock Sandeep out of his calm stupor. Our lives were not exactly going smoothly—there was our son's illness, Komal's constant bickering, and my having to work for money even though I would rather spend time with Amar— yet Sandeep seemed unfazed. As if he were above mortal trauma, as if it didn't matter that I had seen Prakash again, after fifteen long years.

Fifteen years! I couldn't believe that so much time had passed. Prakash seemed unreal, like someone I had met in a dream long gone. But I had seen him again and it didn't seem like a faraway dream anymore. It was closer to a nightmare, and it was suddenly fresh in my mind.

All of it. Every torturous detail.

It was amazing how the past that had become foggy with the passage of time had come into clear focus again because of a small trigger, because I had seen Prakash.

A N J A L I

I stood behind the door of the kitchen and eavesdropped on their conversation. Since I had turned nineteen two years ago, whenever Divya Auntie came home she brought a "maybe" marriage proposal along. She was more interested than my own mother in getting me married. But each time Divya Auntie came with one of her proposals, Mummy listened with eager ears about the boy who would be just perfect for her Anjali.

I moved away from the door when the boiling tea threatened to spill over onto the stove. I switched off the gas and used metal tongs to pour the tea through a plastic sieve into teacups and tried to overhear the conversation in the drawing room.

"The boy is very good-looking, just like Dev Anand in his black-and-white days." Divya Auntie sounded excited and I thought Dev Anand in his black-and-white films looked very handsome. Divya Auntie often drew comparisons between prospective husbands and film stars. She was usually way off the mark.

"He is a captain in the army and you should see him in uniform," Divya Auntie continued, and my interest was piqued. An army officer! Now that was an interesting match. They looked so good in their olive green uniforms, real men, always saying "madam" and "sir."

My mother of course had to find the blemish on the perfect face. "But there is so much travel in the army. One year here and then you have to pack up your life and move. That is so bad for a family . . . though you did a great job with yours."

Divya Auntie, an ex–army officer's wife, snorted as I added sugar to the tea. Three spoons of sugar for Divya Auntie and one for my mother. I stirred slowly so that I wouldn't miss anything being said in the drawing room about the army officer.

"When the match is this good you don't complain about the small things, and there is nothing wrong with moving once in a while," Divya Auntie said. "Our Anjali is very beautiful, and she should marry a nice boy and the Mehra family has a very good reputation. They are very good people. Their friends told us that the boy doesn't drink, doesn't smoke. He doesn't have any bad habits. Imagine being in the army and not drinking? A very nice boy."

I put the teacups on a steel tray along with a small plate of fresh *badam burfi* that I had made just that morning.

"Well, he sounds good, but—"

"But nothing," Divya Auntie snapped. "The boy is here on *chutti*. They don't get a lot of holidays in the army and he is here now to get married. And I think we should start talking, let them both meet, and he . . . he will just fall for her. She is so beautiful."

Since Divya Auntie had for once brought a good proposal

22

for me and said I was beautiful, I refrained from spitting into her tea.

They both became silent as soon as they saw me with the tea. I wondered if they really thought their voices didn't carry to the kitchen, or if they were merely pretending that I didn't know they had been talking about me.

"It is Babli's birthday tomorrow," Divya Auntie said, sipping her tea daintily, giving my mother sly looks. Babli was Divya Auntie's two-year-old granddaughter. "You should come, Anjali."

The army officer was going to be there and I couldn't keep the excitement out of my voice. "I will," I said, biting my lips to stop them from curling into a smile.

"Go early," my mother suggested casually. "You can help Divya Auntie in the kitchen."

I nodded and raced upstairs to my room. I sat down on my bed, heart thumping. He looked like Dev Anand, I thought to myself, as a crazy excitement ripped through me. I was going to be married to an army officer and we would have parties and places to go. And I would have a handsome husband; it was the best thing that could ever happen to me.

Since I had finished my B.A. in English Literature, I wanted to hurry up and get married. Not getting married soon meant that I would have to go to the university to do a master's. My parents had been quite clear about that. I had to at least be "B.A. pass" to get a decent husband, and if I didn't get married a year after I finished the three-year course, I would have to do a master's in a subject of my choice.

"Your chances will be better with an M.A.," Mummy would say. "Better the education, better the husband."

Although that was not always true. Sometimes the girl was too educated and too smart and too independent and she never found a good husband. Men were not interested in a career woman; they wanted a wife, a lady, not some mannish woman who wanted to compete with them.

And I didn't want to study anymore, I wanted to have fun—and what could be more fun than marrying an army officer?

I started to plan the wedding. I knew my friends would be horribly jealous, but then all of them were not fortunate enough to have my good looks. Even though I told everyone that I didn't think I was pretty, I knew otherwise.

I stood in front of the mirror primping my hair. My hair fell straight to my waist and shined if I washed it with the expensive shampoo. I would do that tomorrow, I thought happily and then turned around to open my closet. I went through the hangers, looking for the right sari to wear. There was the yellow silk one with the red border, but that made me look old. It was heavy with gold embroidery and old-fashioned sari-border work. There was the black one with the small golden flowers, but I knew that wouldn't work. Mummy would never agree to a black sari. She would ask me, "Who died?"

I fingered through silk and cotton and finally came upon the sari my grandmother had given to me on my eighteenth birthday. It was ivory silk with tiny blue and gold flowers, and it had a thin dark blue and gold border. I had the perfect blue silk blouse to go with it. It had a low back and made me look sexy. I couldn't wait to enchant my army officer.

The next day I spent hours on my hair, straightening it in the sun as I dried it painstakingly with a thick black comb. I ran the comb through my hair more than a hundred times, while I let the sun seep into the silky strands to remove the moisture from them. My mother came to my room and saw the sari and nodded approvingly. But her face fell with dismay when she saw the blouse.

"No, you can't wear that blouse," she said, horrified that some of my back would be bare.

Didn't she understand? He was an army officer. He was used to seeing modern women, and I needed to look like one to attract his attention.

"This is how they dress these days, Mummy," I said airily. "I like this blouse. It makes me look modern."

Mummy was of course displeased, but she understood that an army officer would want a fashionable wife and she agreed grudgingly to let me wear the blouse.

She lent me her prized pearl necklace and earrings for the occasion. We both knew why I was dressing up for the birthday party of a two-year-old, but we didn't say anything. It was understood that these things were better left unsaid, in case the match didn't work out.

I looked gorgeous.

My eyes were sparkling and expensive rice pearls dangled from my ears, partially hidden by my long straight hair. I wore high-heeled black slippers and my toenails were painted a dark brownish-red. I even wore lipstick—a light shade, of course. It was one thing to look modern and quite another to look like a tramp, and I knew the difference. I was not going to let this opportunity slip by because of the clothes I was wearing. I wanted to look like a modern woman sprinkled with a little bit of the traditional—a good-looking, young, cultured woman, ready to marry an army officer.

Not once did I stop to think why I should want to marry an army officer, or what I would be getting into. I didn't want to look beyond the parties and places I thought I would be going to. It seemed irrelevant. I was raised to be married, and it was time. An army officer seemed glamorous and polished, far from the unsophisticated men Divya Auntie had brought for me before. An army officer meant quality and I wanted to marry quality. A man who didn't fart in public, or stick his finger up his nose, or burp loudly, like my father and uncles did. I wanted a man who was elegant, like the men in the suit ads on television.

I looked at myself in the mirror one last time and gave a dazzling smile. I stood five feet three inches, not too tall and not too short. My hair fell in practiced disarray around my shoulders and my face shined like a thousand-watt bulb. There were advantages to being fair-skinned. Anything I wore, no matter what color it was, no matter the texture of the cloth, looked good on me. And if I applied Fair & Lovely religiously to my face, the sun didn't darken my skin much either.

Yes, I thought, I looked perfect. But I would look even better with an army officer at my side. As I walked the short distance to Divya Auntie's house, I wondered if I should've worn something green in recognition of the army. But then again, I didn't want to be too obvious.

A N J A L I

I made tea for Sandeep and myself. We sat down to enjoy our late evening drink on the open veranda. It was September and Ooty usually started to cool down then. The evenings were not unpleasantly cold, but I was wearing my woolen sweater and socks for warmth. I set my tea aside and walked around the veranda, my mind far away from Sandeep, who was talking about visiting my parents. I stopped in front of a window and saw my dull reflection. How long had it been since I had had the time to see what I looked like? I was perpetually in a hurry, trying to get from Point A to Point B.

Now I stood in front of the window, and saw myself as someone else would see me. I was old and tired, the wrinkles on my face hidden because of the dull light, but that was not what struck me. What struck me was how tired my eyes looked.

This was bound to happen, wasn't it? People grew older and they grew wiser and their eyes reflected their knowledge.

My eyes reflected mine. If I died with my eyes open, people would say, "She lived a weary life." And they would be right.

Even the small gold earrings didn't glitter anymore; neither did my *mangala sutra*. They had all been so bright, so yellow when I first got them. I touched the gold chain of the *mangala sutra*, let my fingers feel the texture of the interlaced gold. When Sandeep and I had married, neither of us had much money, not that things were much different now. We hadn't been able to afford an expensive *mangala sutra*, which hadn't mattered to me. The necklace symbolized marriage—its cost was irrelevant.

I wouldn't have been so flexible when I was twenty-one. I would have demanded the most expensive *mangala sutra* because it was a status symbol and I cared about status symbols in those days.

"What do you think, Anjali?" Sandeep's voice intruded on my thoughts.

"Do you think I am beautiful?" I asked, staring at my reflection.

"Always," he said almost negligently. "How do you feel about going to Hyderabad in the winter holidays?"

I turned around. "I don't know. I don't think Amar in his condition . . . I don't know. How about you?"

Sandeep's eyes glinted with amusement. "What is going on in that head of yours? I just told you that we can take Amar *because* he is feeling a little better."

I bit my lip as I realized what was wrong with me. I had lost my youth and Prakash reminded me of the time when I was carefree and beautiful. Now I had responsibilities, I didn't care what I wore, and I was hardly beautiful. The only man who thought I was beautiful was my husband. I had lost more than that; I had lost the fragrance of my youth, the belief that tomorrow would be a wonderful day. Now I was contaminated with the truth, and the truth was simple—life was sometimes very predictable and tomorrow was going to be just as dull and uneventful as today.

"Anjali?" Sandeep questioned simply. "Are you here, or are you someplace else?"

I turned to face him and smiled because his eyes were laughing at me. He found my day dreams, as he called them, amusing.

"Do you do this when you are teaching in class?" he asked, holding his hand out to me. "You start talking about Hemingway and fall into the other world?"

"No, I don't." I walked to where he was sitting and placed my hand in his. He tugged at it and pulled me onto his lap.

"No," I protested when he held me close. "What will the neighbors say?"

"That the professor and his wife are very much in love."

I looked into Sandeep's eyes. He had taken his glasses off and I was suddenly, crazily happy. Sandeep had the kindest eyes and I found comfort in knowing that they would always be kind. Tomorrow might not have many possibilities, but Sandeep would always be there for and with me.

"And are we very much in love?" I asked impishly.

"Yes."

And that was enough for us. When Amar was born and the doctors had told us that he was a very sick baby, Sandeep told me, "As long as you and I and god are together, we can do anything."

"Why do you want to go to Hyderabad?" I asked patiently. "You know my parents still don't approve of you and . . . I just don't see any reason to go there."

Sandeep hugged me close and leaned his forehead against my breast. "Amar is better, but he is going to get worse. He *is* getting worse, and I just want him to see his grandparents."

My eyes filled with tears because I knew what he meant. He wanted Amar to see his grandparents once more before he died. Our child was going to die and there was nothing anyone could do about it.

No, my mind protested. He wasn't going to die. I told myself I should not even think it. A miracle would happen. He would live—a normal life. It would happen. It had to happen.

"Since your parents won't come here, we should go there. There can't be any pride in this, Anjali. They are old and they should see Amar."

I held Sandeep's face close to my heart and struggled for an emotional balance that was slipping away. How was I supposed to forgive my parents because they were old?

We held each other tightly and tried to forget about our fears and our dreams.

I heard the moan first and an instant later Sandeep heard it, too. We disentangled ourselves and all but ran to our son's room. We always left a small night light on and his bed was enveloped in a red halo.

Amar's eyes were clenched tight and his face was twisted. I sat down on the bed and held his hand. I stroked his forehead and tried to soothe him without waking him up. Sandeep watched from the side of the bed, his face blank, his expression unfathomable as if he didn't want anyone to see what he was feeling. As if he was feeling nothing, even though I could hear his soul weep. He always looked like that when Amar had a nightmare, or a panic attack, or when he was in pain. Amar's arms flailed like the fins of a fish that had been pulled out of water. He shook frantically for a moment and then slid back into sleep.

I continued to hold his hand, cursing fate for what had been done to our son, and I felt anger surge through me like it was new and fresh. Its taste was acrid and once again I hated Prakash, effortlessly and hungrily.

Not seeing him for fifteen years had eased the pain and the anger. But now he was here, just a few kilometers away, sleeping with his pretty wife, not knowing what he had done to me, to my son. Prakash had no idea what we had been through and how much he was to blame.

My favorite author without doubt was Saki, also known as H. H. Munro. I loved his quirky short stories and took pleasure in teaching my students to love them, too. We followed the syllabus provided by the school board, but I always added a short story here and a short story there from Saki's delectable collection.

I enjoyed teaching ninth grade English. When I was young I hadn't paid any attention to what I was reading. Life was a series of Mills & Boon novels, full of fantasy, romance, and unconditionally horrible chauvinistic men. Then one day I discovered Graham Greene and his *The End of the Affair*. I was smitten. Here was beautiful writing. It probably had not happened overnight—I had not changed from an airhead to a serious woman in a flash. It had taken time and it had taken several bad experiences. I grew up and growing up for me had also meant discovering something new to enjoy and love. Literature had given me a means to end the drudgery of my superficial life where I was more interested in finding a husband than finding myself.

As I did my master's in education, I knew I wanted to teach English. I wanted everyone to read good literature and enjoy it the way I did. I didn't want them to end up in a wasteland of contemporary thriller fiction. I succeeded with some, while others hid Danielle Steele and Sidney Sheldon novels in between the pages of their textbooks.

I also read to Amar, who at twelve knew Shakespeare and had read his work. He could quote Portia in the last court scene of *The Merchant of Venice*, he loved Puck from *A Midsummer Night's Dream*, and thought *Romeo and Juliet* was boring. He loved reading Phantom comics and enjoyed listening to old Hindi film songs. He broke my heart. I knew he tried to do more because he knew he didn't have much time. He loved old Mohammad Rafi and Kishore Kumar songs and played their records again and again on an old LP I had bought from a used music store in my university days.

He was my favorite student.

It was a few days after meeting Prakash that I met him again. I was in the teachers' staff room at school and Mrs. Gujjar, who taught math to ninth- and tenth-grade students, was there as well, coughing loudly into a dirty white handkerchief.

"*Arrey,* Anjali, there is someone looking for you," she said, blowing her nose. "Some army officer."

I stiffened and then nodded slowly. "Where is he now?"

"I sent him to your class, and he said that he would come back if you were not there." Mrs. Gujjar took a deep raspy breath and sighed. "This climate is killing me. I am going to get TB if I live here any longer. But my husband won't get a transfer for another year. These government jobs are just . . . terrible. He works so hard in that post office and they pay him peanuts and . . . we have to live here, in this cold pit."

I sat down at my desk, put my papers away, and waited. My feet tapped against the cement floor keeping time. Prakash was here to see me and even though I tried, I couldn't stop the goose bumps from sprouting all over my arms. As I wrapped my shawl tightly around my shoulders, I heard his boots thumping on the floor right behind me.

I stood up unsteadily and turned. *"Namaste,"* I all but whispered.

It seemed so formal to say that to him, but Mrs. Gujjar was in the room, so I could hardly be anything but formal. Ooty was a small place and the last thing I needed was for people at school to talk about Professor Sharma's wife and the army officer.

"Can I speak with you?" he asked, and I looked at Mrs. Gujjar from the corner of my eye. She was surreptitiously watching us, trying to draw every piece of information she could from our conversation.

"Of course," I said with forced enthusiasm. "Ah . . . please . . . ah . . . we can sit . . . ."

Mrs. Gujjar showed no signs of leaving the staff room, and Prakash shifted on his feet uneasily. "How about out there?" He pointed to the banyan tree right outside the staff room and I sighed. This would be all over Ooty soon—*an army officer came to see Anjali Sharma and they talked under the tree. . . .*

"I am so sorry, I hope I didn't say anything wrong." Prakash sounded contrite.

I ignored his feeble apology. "Why are you here?" I demanded.

"I am sorry about yesterday. I just didn't know what to tell Indu about you."

Indu for Indira. Anju for Anjali.

"I don't care what you tell your wife. I don't know why you are here."

"You got married," he said suddenly.

"So did you," I pointed out. "If you don't mind . . ." I started to turn back to leave, but I stopped when he spoke.

"I wanted to see you. . . . How are you?" His Adam's apple bobbed as he swallowed.

"I am fine," I snapped.

"Who did you marry?"

Was this curiosity or concern?

"How does it matter?" I was appalled at his audacity to come here and pry into my personal life. If I hadn't seen his wife yesterday, I would be curious, too, but I had and I wasn't anymore. "He is a math professor at the College of Computer Studies. He is . . . just who he is. Why do you care?"

Prakash was a brigadier now. I noticed the stars on his shoulder flaps. He didn't have any new medals, but there hadn't been any new wars. His uniform was the same as it had always been. Short-sleeve shirt, pants that were always perfectly ironed, and shoes that were polished so well you could see your reflection in them.

"I just . . . I felt like things were hanging after yesterday."

"Things have been hanging for fifteen years, Prakash," I said, not giving him an inch. This was how my fantasy had been. He would want to talk to me and I would play the arrogant queen. After Amar's nightmare episode last night, I was haughtier than ever.

"I know."

"No, you don't. And if you don't mind, please don't come here again. What will people think? I care about my reputation. I have a family, a husband, a son, and I can't just talk to strange men."

"But I am not a strange man," he said unsteadily.

"You are a strange man because I don't really know you. Now if you will excuse me . . ."

"I just wanted to say I was sorry."

I stifled the tears and nodded hastily before blindly stumbling back to the staff room, leaving Prakash standing alone under the banyan tree.

I was shaking with anger and relief. He had apologized, and if I had not been caught so off guard, I would have demanded what he was voluntarily apologizing for.

I was sorry, too. Sorry that he was such a miserable excuse for a man. Sorry that I had loved him once and *really* sorry that I had ever been married to him.

A N J A L I

All I could think when Divya Auntie introduced me to Captain Prakash Mehra was that he was even better looking than Dev Anand. He was an engineer in the Electrical and Mechanical Engineers Corps. His hair was cut in a stern crew cut, but his face was full of mischief and life. He had been singing nursery rhymes with Babli and her friends when I entered Divya Auntie's house. When he saw me, he stood up and smiled.

That was all it took to get stars in my eyes.

Divya Auntie's house was a typical ex–army officer's house. There were things from everywhere: a wooden idol of Krishna from Baroda, a cane screen from Assam, beautiful hand-woven carpets from Nepal, a huge brass tank barrel that Divya Auntie had arranged dry flowers in, and furniture collected from all over the country.

Since two-year-olds were unpredictable, Divya Auntie had moved the glass vases and glass tea trolley and had replaced them with plastic toys and balloons. I always thought that since

Divya Auntie's husband had retired as a brigadier, her house exuded wealth and sophistication. It was not *real* wealth, but she managed to make her drawing room and the rest of her house look like they belonged to a rich family. Somehow army wives knew how to do that. They had class and elegance, which we civilians seemed to lack.

Divya Auntie was an amateur painter, and on the off-white walls of the drawing room hung vivid paintings of bullock carts and villages, of women carrying earthen pots on their heads, and, in the painting that I liked most, Omar Khayyám lay luxuriously under a tree, holding an ornate glass of wine, while a beautiful woman sat beside him playing the harp.

Divya Auntie had promised to give me old Omar as a wedding gift. After seeing Prakash, I yearned for that painting as I had never before.

"What do you want to do now that you have finished your B.A.? Work? Go back for an M.A.?" Prakash asked, and I smiled gently and shrugged. It was not important for me to go to work or get a better education. I had other plans, glorious plans. I would take care of my husband, my house, and my children. I would cook great meals and invite people for dinner. In the army everyone threw big parties and I would make it my job to be the perfect hostess.

"Where are you posted now?" I asked, changing the subject. Men liked to talk about themselves and I wanted to know more about him.

"I just got my transfer papers to go to Bhopal. There is an EME Center there. I was in Udhampur before that."

"Udhampur?" I couldn't contain my joy. He had been to places I hadn't even heard of before.

"It's in Jammu and Kashmir, about fifty kilometers above Jammu. It's a nice place, close to Srinagar."

"It must be fun to travel and see new places," I said playing with the edge of my sari. I leaned against the wall of the balcony, where Divya Auntie had sent us to "talk." Some children peeped through the glass doors and then slithered away as Divya Auntie stood guard.

"Yes, it is. Do you like to travel?"

My eyes hit the floor. "Act demurely in front of a man," my grandmother would always say. I wanted to be Mrs. Prakash Mehra, but I couldn't be overt; I couldn't just tell him that he was what I wanted. What if he wasn't interested?

"I love to travel," I said, raising my eyes slowly and looking into his with confidence. "I haven't done much though. Just a little. I went to Bombay for a wedding last year and . . . a friend of mine got married in Madras a month ago."

"In the army there is constant moving," Prakash seemed to warn me. "You think you could deal with constant moving?"

I was dumbfounded. He was so direct. He was almost proposing to me and that was not how marriage proposals were made. He first had to speak with his parents and they would speak with my parents and then the matter would be arranged. Ordinary men didn't speak like this, only an army officer did, I thought happily. My lips broke into a genuine smile.

"I could deal with it very easily," I said.

That was all it took. A few minutes of conversation and the date of the marriage was fixed.

⤏ F I V E

A N J A L I

I was still seething when I got home. How dare he come to my school and embarrass me? Mrs. Gujjar had asked all sorts of questions after Prakash left . . .

Who is he?
How do you know him?
Does your husband know him?
Does your husband know *you* know him?
Is he an old friend?
How long since you've known him?

I had answered each question patiently and unconvincingly. By the time I got out of my afternoon class, everyone in the staff room wanted to know about the brigadier who had come to see me. If I had said ex-husband, they all would have shut up and it would have also started nonstop gossip. No one in the school knew I had been married to someone else besides Sandeep.

If people at school found out that I was a divorcée and that I had spoken to my ex-husband again, the scandal would force us to leave Ooty. This was a small city and our circle was even smaller as he was a professor and I was a teacher. Everyone in the education community knew everyone; nothing went unnoticed, definitely not an army officer in full uniform looking for a teacher in her school.

It was when my friend, Mrs. Rita Chaddha, a geography teacher, wanted to know who Prakash was, that I lost my temper. Rita and I were friends (well, as close as we could be). We had known each other for the past four years since she and her husband had moved to Ooty. Our social interaction was limited to the spare time we had during school hours. We didn't share secrets, but she knew how things were in my house, who Komal was, everyday stuff. And I knew about her life, how much money her husband spent on drinking and why she sometimes sported a black eye.

Rita had been astounded when I told her to mind her own business. A man wanted to speak with me and I knew him from long ago, why was that such a big issue? It was Rita's response that shook me up.

"You look like you did something wrong and that is the issue."

I was glad when I heard the school bell ring. I didn't wait for the school bus as usual, even though I knew it would raise eyebrows. I had had enough silent accusations for one day. Hopefully, something else would happen the next day and they would forget about Prakash.

I walked the two kilometers home, dragging my feet, angry and scared. Would it become a big issue? Had *I* made it a big issue?

It was startling to know that the society I lived in was so fragile and my place in it was contingent on innumerable things.

As soon as I got home I heard Komal calling out to me. I wished she would nag me right now because I would, I definitely would, snap her head off. I had been patient long enough with too many people and all I got in return was a long walk back from school.

"The school bus came an hour ago—"

"I am not in the mood," I snapped, and walked past her into the house.

"Mala's sister's friend, Shobha, whose brother's wife teaches in your school, said that some army officer came to see you." Komal's hands were curled into fists and rested on her waist. Her eyes were suspicious, her chin adamantly rigid, as if whatever I had to say would not change her mind.

I was not surprised by her behavior; what surprised me was how fast the news had spread.

I glared back at her and decided to outstare her. I had put up with enough. I was not a fifteen-year-old adolescent who had to be warned against evil men. I was old enough to know whom I could speak with and when.

"You told everyone that he is an old *friend*," Komal accused. We stared at each other with unblinking eyes in contest.

I blinked.

What was the point? Komal had made up her mind

anyway. I walked to Amar's room and knocked gently. His voice (it sounded strong) welcomed me in.

I leaned down and kissed him on the forehead. He looked healthy today. He didn't look like he was ready to spring out of bed like all children his age, but in his case, it was relative. Today his pallor was not yellow, even though it was not rosy. His eyes were shining and didn't look . . . dead.

"How have you been today?" I asked, sitting next to him on the bed after I shut the door on Komal, who had been following me to probably demand more answers regarding the army officer.

"I started reading *Catch-22*," he said with a broad smile. "I think I understand some of it."

I smiled. He probably did. My genius son. I had picked it up for him a few days ago from the library. They had started showing the television series *M*A*S*H* on cable TV, and we had talked about the Korean War. I mentioned *Catch-22* and he said he wanted to read it.

"It *is* funny and I am glad you find it funny, too."

"I said I understood some of it, not that I found it funny," he corrected me, and I laughed.

Amar was fascinated by stories and read as many books as he could. Every Sunday, Amar would go to the library with Sandeep or me, and we would bring back dozens of books. By the end of the week he had either read or browsed through all of them. If he was like the other children his age, he probably would go to school and learn like all normal children. But Amar couldn't go to school so Sandeep and I tried to play the role of tutor for him. But it was difficult to impose formal education on him when he was fighting for his life.

"Do you feel like a walk?" I asked him. We tried to get him out of the house every day, so that the sun would kiss him and he would get some fresh air. Amar got into the wheelchair and looked up at me.

"Maybe I can walk today," he suggested, his eyes pleading.

"We won't go too far," I agreed.

Anything he wanted, I would give if I could. If he wanted to walk, then he would walk. I also knew that each time he walked, he tired in a few minutes, and sometimes I had to carry him back home.

I helped him into a sweater and wrapped his woolen shawl around him. He was tall, my son, like Sandeep, and he was beautiful. When he grew up to be a man, Sandeep and I would have to beat eager, lovesick girls away with sticks.

Our walk entailed a small twirl around our garden. If Amar was in his wheelchair, I usually took him to the park half a kilometer away, where we would sit and talk. We would buy roasted peanuts from the vendor who sold them in newspaper cones.

He refused to hold on to me as he walked around the garden. He bent down awkwardly to touch an errant rose bud, which would probably die before it could bloom. It was September, not the right month for roses.

By the time Sandeep got home, Amar was fast asleep. The walk had tired him and he had barely managed to eat the *dal* and rice I mixed for him when we got back. I fed him and then helped him take a warm bath before putting him to bed. It was like he was still a baby, and in so many physical ways he still was. But Amar fought, fought hard to do the things twelve-year-olds were supposed to do. He understood the limitations of his body, yet I could see him struggle to understand why this was happening to him. Why couldn't he go to school like the others? And why couldn't he take a walk without feeling the life wheeze out of him?

Komal and I were watching the Hindi news on television when Sandeep came home. The atmosphere was chilly and I knew Sandeep picked up on it as soon as he saw our grouchy faces.

I went into the kitchen and started to make tea, wanting privacy to talk to him about Prakash before Komal started her nagging routine.

But Komal was a step ahead of me. I heard her shrill voice tell him about the army officer I was "gallivanting" with. I was glad that no one in Sandeep's family knew about my first marriage. I had told Sandeep about Prakash in the beginning, long before we fell in love. He'd told me that my past was my business and he couldn't and wouldn't judge me for it.

"Before you say anything . . ." I held up my hand as soon as Sandeep stepped into the kitchen.

"Prakash came to see you in school," he supplied warmly, and kissed me just as warmly on the mouth.

"I didn't invite him," I told him belligerently.

"It wouldn't matter even if you did," he said, sitting down on the kitchen chair. "He is from your past and . . . you can't just ignore how you feel about him."

I flew into a rage. "I feel nothing for him but distaste and I told him that. How dare you suggest—"

"I suggest nothing," he interrupted smoothly, his eyes alight with amusement. "Why are you so defensive? He came to meet you. I don't care, so why do you?"

I had no idea why. In a way I felt guilty because I had wanted to see Prakash again after meeting him in the market.

"He came to apologize."

"Hmm."

"I didn't ask him for what," I said, handing him his cup of tea. "I made *dal* and cauliflower *sabzi* for dinner. I just have to cook the rice. It will take fifteen minutes."

"Why don't you put the rice on the stove and then come outside with me?"

I did as he said. I ignored the triumphant look Komal gave me as we walked past her to go to the veranda. The woman knew nothing about her brother. Sandeep would never suspect me or accuse me; he was a fair man who wouldn't jump to conclusions without knowing all the facts.

"Amar's always asleep when I come home," he complained. "I only get to see him on Sundays now. It will be nice to spend more time with him in the winter holidays."

"He wanted to walk today. That's why he fell asleep so soon," I told him.

We sat next to each other in the wicker chairs, looking straight ahead into the night. He didn't say anything and soon I was uncomfortable with the silence.

"About Prakash—" I began.

"I don't want to talk about Prakash," Sandeep groaned. "I just want to be with you for a while. I am tired and I don't want to discuss your ex-husband and his motives."

45

I wanted to yell at him again, but he did look tired and he was right, there was nothing to say. Prakash came to see me and apologized, end of story.

"I am buying train tickets for Hyderabad," Sandeep said after another period of silence.

I sighed. "Let me write a letter to my mother and see if they will come here. I don't want to tire Amar more than necessary."

Sandeep nodded in agreement.

"They gave me a tough time at school," I blurted out, my eyes filled with tears. "I feel like I have committed some crime and you don't even want to talk about it because you think I have."

"You have what?"

"Committed a crime."

Sandeep laughed and stood up. He held his hand out to me and pulled me to my feet into his arms. He rocked me gently and we stood there for a long time, listening to the crickets and the whistle of a train far away. The sounds of the night blended into each other and soothed me. It didn't matter that Prakash was back in my life, or that Mrs. Gujjar had interrogated me. It was enough to have Sandeep.

We stood there until we heard the sharp whistle of the pressure cooker indicating the rice was done.

After dinner Komal went to her room, unhappy that Sandeep didn't seem interested in the man who had come to see me. We checked on Amar, who was blissfully sleeping, before we went to bed.

Our bedroom was right next to Amar's. I liked it because it was ours. This was something Sandeep and I shared in its en-

tirety. The cupboard had my clothes and his. In the small bathroom attached to our room—the landlord had told us what a
luxury it was to have our very own bathroom—our tooth-
brushes lay next to each other. My Pond's powder sat next to
his shaving cream, my razor touched his, his cologne rested
against my perfume bottle. Just like our lives, our bedroom en-
twined us together.

Sandeep read the newspaper and I read through the next
day's lesson plan. We lay in bed reading, enjoying each other's
presence without being intrusive.

Like I usually did, I put my textbook away and yanked the
newspaper from Sandeep. He pushed his reading glasses up his
nose and looked at me in mock enquiry. I smiled and he
turned out the lights.

Sex with Sandeep has always been *nice*. A term the ro-
mantics detest to use, but I was not a romantic anymore. We
made love with relaxed passion, as if we had all the time in the
world. He took my clothes off slowly and I watched as he took
his off. It was easy to make love with Sandeep because he was
patient, kind, and generous. Bells didn't go off and the earth
didn't shake, but I climaxed pleasantly.

We were never caught in the throes of passion. Sandeep
never dragged me down to the floor and ravished me. We
never had sex half-clothed because there was no reason for
haste.

He touched my nipples gently and even though I sometimes wanted him to exert more pressure, I didn't ask him to. It
was comforting to lie back and enjoy his hands on me. Other
times he lay back to let me have my way with him.

When I came, he usually kissed me or clamped his hand

on my mouth to silence me. The walls were thin, the house small, and both Komal and Amar could hear us. As far as unabashed passion went, my small squeaks were the only proof of it. Sandeep was always quiet. Besides his accelerated breathing nothing gave him away.

I held him after he was done, stroking his shoulders as he got his breath back. We had it almost down to a science, a procedure, not that we minded.

We lay in each other's arms and talked after we made love. He told me how beautiful I was, and how he loved to make love to me. I told him how I liked to feel him inside me. I kissed his chin, he played with a nipple. I ran my foot against his leg, he stroked my inner thighs. I caressed his softening erection and he played with my clitoris.

The caresses were warm and gentle, just like our relationship.

A N J A L I

The first night!

I had expected amazing lovemaking, just like in the books, and I had expected the man to be gentle and wonderful, a teacher. I was a virgin, and I was warned about the pain during sex for the first time. I ignored it believing that women had pain when the men didn't arouse them. Prakash Mehra was going to arouse me before he breached my womanhood. I was convinced of that. He was a gentleman and he always held the door open for me. Why would he be different during sex?

The first night after the wedding, like most first nights, despite what I had wanted it to be, was a nightmare. Sex that had seemed so beautiful in books and in my imagination turned out to be a rutting session that I didn't want to go through ever again. To me the first night was the first time I would have sex; to Prakash it was probably a simple act of consummation.

I had worn a light pink silk nightgown for the occasion. I was horribly tired after the long five-day wedding. Everything had been chaotic and I had felt like a doll as I was paraded in front of everyone. Prakash's family members came one by one to see if maybe, despite the rumors, I was actually ugly. His grandmother made me open my mouth to check my teeth, while his great-aunt made me walk just to make sure there was nothing wrong with my legs. All this after the wedding had begun. They all wanted to make sure Prakash was getting an appropriate wife.

My parents had spent an exorbitant amount of money on our lavish wedding. Thousands of pictures were taken by a professional photographer hired to catch every memory, every nuance of the wedding, in color. Everything had been done according to scripture and tradition; the only problem had been Prakash. He had issues with everything. Instead of just going through all the ceremonies, he questioned all of them. He had tried to convince his parents and mine that the wedding should be a small affair, but no one listened to him. When he asked me if I wanted a large wedding, I had nodded sheepishly. I was twenty-one, I wanted to show off, and I didn't know any better. That enraged him and we had our first fight before we walked around the fire seven times.

We were in my parents' living room and he walked out in midsentence—my midsentence. Half an hour later he came back and apologized. I started to cry and he brushed my tears. It was the first time we kissed. I had been shocked by his audacity. After all, this kind of kissing was done after the marriage ceremony. His hands had roamed my body and he had touched my breasts. I was excited but embarrassed, too. We were both saved from our passions when my mother walked into the room. I think she knew what we had been doing, but she pretended not to.

We spent our first night as husband and wife in his parents' house, as tradition demanded. Prakash's old bedroom had been decorated for the event. His mother had painstakingly sprinkled rose petals on the white sheets of a newly purchased double bed and had sprayed a cloying rose perfume around the whole room.

An auspicious time had been picked out for the first-night ritual of copulation, and I was supposed to be ready for my husband. My mother installed me in the bedroom an hour before Prakash was supposed to be there. She made sure my nightgown was not crumpled and complained about my drooping eyes, then left me alone to wait for my future.

When Prakash entered the room I could smell alcohol on his breath. I instantly wanted to throw a tantrum about it, but this was our wedding night and I didn't want him to think I was a shrew. I realized then that I knew nothing about Prakash, and that he knew nothing about me. Divya Auntie had said that he didn't drink alcohol and she was obviously mistaken, which meant that he was a mystery and every day would be a revelation. It was intimidating and exciting. We had a lifetime to get to know one another and I couldn't wait for the lifetime to begin.

As soon as he closed the door behind him he started taking his clothes off. The enormity of what was to happen struck me. All my life my parents had worked toward protecting my virginity. Now this man, a veritable stranger, would breach my virginity and honor and my parents were happy about it because he had tied a *mangala sutra* around my neck.

I clamped my mouth shut when Prakash sat down on the bed, crushing rose petals, and started to remove his underwear. I had never seen a naked man in my life. His body was hairy and his penis . . . I looked away. It was sticking out of his body and it looked big. I knew the basics of sex and my mother, despite my protests, had explained the process. Her rules were simple: lie down and let *him* do whatever he wants to do.

"A woman doesn't have to enjoy sex. There is nothing to enjoy really. It is the means to have a baby and men like it," she had said.

My mother's explanation aside, I had started taking birth control pills two weeks before the wedding. Prakash had told me that he didn't want children for at least one year after the wedding, and I agreed. It would be like one long honeymoon, my delusional brain deduced.

He sat next to me on the bed, naked. "Are you scared?" he asked politely, and I nodded, not looking at him at all.

"You'll get used to it."

I looked up then. "Have you done it before?"

He seemed angry and uncomfortable with my question. "I am sorry," I immediately soothed. "It was a stupid question."

The anger left his eyes as soon as I apologized. But I had my answer. My army officer had done this before. I should've been angry, and I was, but I was also excited. He was an experienced man; he would know how to do it right. Just like the tall, dark, and handsome men in romance novels.

His hands found their way to the ties of my nightgown and I held my breath. He slipped the shoulder straps down my arms and the nightgown slithered to my waist and almost immediately his hands launched an attack on my breasts. I was too nervous to be aroused or excited. I kept wondering why he didn't kiss me. The kissing after our fight had been fun. This part, however, scared the living daylights out of me.

He pushed me onto the bed and removed my nightgown. My white panties followed. My thighs instantly crossed, trying to protect my virtue. Prakash seemed too far gone to care what I felt and, in less than a minute after my panties had joined the nightgown on the floor, my army officer forced himself inside me, while I cried bloody murder.

He pounded in and out and I kept crying. His eyes were closed and his breathing was harsh. Finally, he heaved and groaned and then fell over my body. To make matters worse he was heavy. I tried to push him off me gently, not wanting to insult him in any way. I was his wife and this is what I had to put up with. My mother was right, damn her.

He moved on his own accord in a few minutes. He slumped on the bed on his stomach and opened his eyes to look at me.

"Good night," he said politely, and fell asleep.

I stared at him, hoping he wasn't sleeping. Was this it? This was sex? Where was the romance I was promised in the Mills & Boon novels? I wanted an explanation! But he started snoring, and all my shaking him did was stop the snores for a while.

A N J A L I

It was a Sunday when I saw her again. In the market, wearing the same woolen coat. This time, she carried a small dark leather hand purse and Prakash was not with her.

Sandeep patted my shoulder. "Do you want to buy *bhindi* or not?"

I looked at the plump okra and nodded. "Two kilos," I mumbled at the vendor, and picked up the weights he was using to check if they were lighter than they were supposed to be.

"I am not a cheat, *Memsaab*." The vendor smiled, showing his cracked and yellowed teeth. "Everything here is—"

"I know how everything is here," I snapped. "And put that *bhindi* you took out back on the plate."

I felt unsettled. The market was turning into a "meet your past" carnival booth.

Sandeep put the okra in a cloth bag and paid the vendor. We surveyed the other shops and avoided banana peels and rotten vegetables on the cobbled stones as we walked around the market.

"Fruit," I said, when Sandeep asked what else we needed. "Amar asked for an apple yesterday and we didn't have any."

"Sure . . . where are the apples?" Sandeep asked, looking around.

"There," I pointed out.

"Where?" he asked, not looking exactly where I was pointing.

"There," I said in exasperation. "Can't you see? Are you blind?"

Sandeep stopped me from moving by putting his hand under my elbow. "What is the matter with you? You were fine a minute ago and now you are the incarnation of Durga Ma."

I swallowed uneasily. How much could I tell him? Should I tell him? I knew I would eventually tell him the truth, one way or the other.

"Are you okay?" he persisted, so I decided to tell him what the problem was.

"I . . . just . . . saw his wife."

"Where?" Sandeep looked around and I jerked my eyebrows in her direction. "Very pretty," he said, then turned toward me. "Of course, she doesn't hold a candle to your beauty."

"Of course," I said sarcastically.

"They live here, Anjali. We are going to keep seeing them in the market, the cinema, somewhere or other," he cautioned. "Are you going to be in a bad mood each time it happens?"

I understood what he was saying, but I didn't think he understood how I felt. It was envy, pure and simple. That was supposed to be my life. I was supposed to be an army officer's wife. I was supposed to be wearing the pretty saris and carry-ing the expensive purses. I was supposed to be going to all the parties and living the frivolous life; instead I was living a life that didn't compare to what I had thought I wanted. I felt guilty as soon as I thought that. I loved Sandeep and I was thankful that I was not married to Prakash anymore. That was reality. In my head, however, I wanted to be someone else; I wanted to have flights of fantasy like I did when I was twenty-one.

"No, I am not going to be in a bad mood because of her or him," I said, and went toward the apple vendor.

Sandeep and I walked back home in silence. I knew he was angry—he only fell that silent when he was angry.

❧ E I G H T

S A N D E E P

I never understood why Anjali was still so obsessed with Prakash.

She said she hated him, didn't feel any warmth for him, and most of the time she believed herself, I think, but deep down I knew she missed her life with him. Life with me was simple and predictable. I was a professor. I talked about math and I talked about making ends meet by tutoring rich children on the side. Our son was sick and each day we prayed for a miracle that would let him live longer, spend more time in this world. Other days we prayed for his pain to go away, for him to sleep peacefully throughout the night. We prayed that he would walk around the garden without tiring himself. And added to all that, my sister lived with us.

It was probably the total opposite of what Anjali expected from life. She had wanted to be an army officer's wife with all its glamour, and here she was married to our problems and to me.

As we walked back home from the vegetable bazaar, I

wondered about the past and the present. Since Prakash had appeared in Ooty, Anjali seemed more agitated, more stressed, and somehow, more happy. It was as if she had been waiting for this day, and now that it was here she was going to indulge in it. Prakash had apologized to her and I knew that it meant more to her than she was making out of it.

Seeing his wife had torn her up with jealousy. She wasn't jealous because I thought his wife was pretty; she was jealous because Prakash's wife was . . . well, Prakash's wife.

I couldn't even argue with her; after all, she had always been honest with me. Always told me her secrets, no matter how dark they were, so how could I tell her that her feelings hurt me? She didn't even know she felt the things that hurt me. Her eyes lit up at the name of Prakash, but I didn't know if it was with anger or with pleasure.

She had loved him once, deeply, and I was tortured with jealousy at times. Yet I wouldn't change a thing. This is what made Anjali the woman I love. Her vivacity, her love for life, and her fierce passion made Anjali, Anjali—and I could not hold that against her.

But I was tormented nevertheless. When Komal told me an army officer came to see Anjali in school, the jolt had been worth a million volts, but I stayed calm. My wife was a lot of things; a cheat she was not. She would leave me before she cheated on me and sometimes I worried that she would do both.

Oh, I knew we loved each other and that she took her marriage vows just as seriously as I took mine. But there was Prakash in the past, and he kept peeping into our lives each time Anjali's body remembered the Bhopal gas tragedy, and now he lived just a few kilometers away.

Anjali didn't know this, but I had seen her first wedding photo album. It had been buried under books and papers in some long forgotten box in the attic. It had been a depressing day when I had been sifting through the junk from our pasts. The gold on red leather, the words PRAKASH WEDS ANJALI flashed, ensnared me.

She had been a gorgeous bride, all bright-eyed and fresh, and he had been handsome. He probably still was. I was considered "nice" looking, hardly the material used in men's suit commercials on television. My hair was graying, though I still had most of it. At forty-five I was no catch, and I had been no catch at thirty-one either when I met Anjali.

Prakash on the other hand looked perfect, perfect for her. Did she feel that she had made the wrong choice with me? I wondered about that, too, but the insecurities didn't burden my life. They raised their ugly head whenever she mentioned Prakash and I remembered the one picture from the album that was sealed in my memory. He was holding Anjali's hand at the reception and she was looking into his eyes. She was looking at him like he was the only man in the entire world, and while they had been married, he *had* been the only man for her in the entire world.

I felt like I was the consolation prize. It wasn't just about good looks. It was more the aura Anjali associated army officers with. I had met several men and women like Anjali, who thought that army officers were perfect men. Patriotic, well dressed, and more Western than most of us civilian saps. Especially after a war or a publicized border skirmish, army officers looked even better to the public. To Anjali, they were demigods, or at least they had been. Now she seemed to feel the opposite, and even though I believed her, I had my doubts. Small, inconsequential, almost unthinkable doubts.

Prakash was her past and now he was in her present and I was terrified of what might happen.

Komal was in Amar's room when we got home and I could hear them talking. Despite how she was with Anjali, my sister loved Amar. She sat with him, cared for him, and allowed both of us to have jobs. Jobs that brought the money necessary to keep Amar alive and all of us afloat. Komal didn't cook often, which bothered Anjali. But Anjali didn't complain and I appreciated her for that. She came home tired and immediately started to cook every day. On Sundays she cooked lavish meals, coaxing Amar to taste new dishes.

She worked very hard at home and at work. Before she left for school every morning, Anjali swept the house, her back curved as she used the soft broom to clean out the day's debris from the tiled floors of our rented home.

Anjali had wanted the house as soon as we saw it. It had three bedrooms. Amar's and ours were next to each other and a bathroom was between Amar's and Komal's bedrooms. And the price was just right for us. There were problems—the leaky roof in the kitchen, the cracked tiles in our bathroom, and some of the windows wouldn't open and some wouldn't close properly. But the house had a garden and Anjali wanted Amar to be close to that. She wanted him to step out of the house to smell the freshly cut grass, touch the roses, soak in the sunlight, and bond with nature.

I loved the garden, the flowers, and the lawn. I pulled the weeds, watered the plants and cared for them, made sure they stayed alive through the season. In winters when the frost covered the grass in the lawn and the rose bushes shriveled, we still sat on the veranda, looking at our little piece of paradise.

Anjali wanted her *own* house; I knew that. She wanted us to buy a home, but she didn't once complain about the lack of funds that would allow us to do so. Compared to other wives, Anjali had never asked for one thing and that agitated me more than anything else did. Did she not ask me for anything because she knew I couldn't afford it?

I had seen her wedding pictures, the lush jewelry she wore and now didn't have. After the divorce, the jewelry had given her the financial freedom to get an education so that she could stand on her own feet. I couldn't replace her jewelry then and I couldn't now and that made me feel impotent. When we went to weddings, her hands were the barest and her neck the one with the lightest gold. I couldn't give her material comforts, and even though I didn't *really* believe that the man should be the only breadwinner, I knew that was how she had been raised. I wondered if she looked at me and saw a lesser man. A man who needed his wife to work to pay the bills. Anjali liked to teach, but I wish she didn't have to do it. I wish she could spend her days with Amar.

When Anjali went to check on Amar, I washed the tomatoes and okra we had bought at the market and left them to dry on a wooden board. Amar loved Anjali's okra curry, and that's why she made it as often as the prices and the season would allow it. My son was smart and understood the financial intricacies of our lives. He told Anjali that if he ate okra curry too often he would stop enjoying it and he wanted to continue to like it. Anjali had laughed with him and then cried with me. It was not fair, she had said, that a little boy knew what his parents' limitations were. Parents are supposed to be infallible, perfect creatures, but Anjali felt we were bad parents because our son knew we were fallible. It was not because we couldn't afford okra every day; it was because we couldn't protect our son and save him from his own body.

Each day I hoped Amar was gaining strength and each day I was reminded this child of mine had been given less than a few years to live when he was born. Anjali hadn't known that the effects of that deadly night in Bhopal would lead to a child with a weak heart and weak lungs. She hadn't known and because of that even though I wanted to blame her for our son sometimes, I couldn't. It wouldn't be fair and above all else I wanted to be a fair man.

But how could a husband be fair, when his wife's eyes brightened at the mention of the man who was to blame for their son's hasty life?

Anjali came into the kitchen and wrapped her arms around me, her face leaning against my back.

"Are you angry?" she asked.

I shook my head and turned around. I kissed her softly on the mouth and shook my head again. "About what?"

"About his wife?"

I wrinkled my nose in affected confusion. "I should be angry that he has a wife?"

She stuck her tongue out playfully and genuinely laughed. That's what I was good at, at making her smile even when she didn't want to, even when she thought she couldn't. It didn't matter that Prakash was in her past when I held her in my arms. This beautiful, wonderful, strong woman was mine. She was my wife and I loved her, loved her for who she was, and who she wasn't.

"Do you want me to cook tonight?" I asked, as I usually did on weekends, and she shook her head, as she usually did.

I would do anything for her, but I didn't think she realized that. If the time came and she wanted to leave me for a better life, I wouldn't stop her. For all that she had been through, I wanted her to be happy. But happiness was elusive; like a chimera it slipped through our fingers. A year after we got married we had Amar. The ecstasy of having a child was shadowed by the pronouncements of the doctors. We had spent all our savings, everything we had, which was not much, in finding better doctors in the hope that they would tell us that Amar was all right and that the other doctors were wrong. But the writing was on the wall; Amar didn't have much time. So we dragged each minute as long as we could and hoped for that unlikely miracle to occur—for Amar to wake up one morning and say, "I am fine," and mean it.

She leaned away from me, frowning. "Why don't you hate him?"

She had asked that question several times before. I hated Prakash, I most certainly did. He had touched my wife's lithe body, he had kissed her wide mouth, he had caressed her breasts. The possessiveness of those acts made me cringe with jealousy. Prakash had married her in a lavish wedding; I hadn't. Our wedding had been a simple, sign-on-this-piece-of-paper affair. She had seemed happy, enthralled, but I wondered if she compared the two weddings. And if she did, did I fail miserably?

"Hate is a very strong emotion," I said calmly. It was not a complete lie. I would hate her first husband, whoever he was, but I didn't know if I hated Prakash, the man. He had been young, just twenty-five when he married her. Being married at a young age, even though by the standards of society he was old enough to be married and have a couple of children, must have been difficult. But he had made more mistakes than his age could excuse. Adultery was not something I condoned, but hate was too strong an emotion to subject oneself to, even for adultery.

"Do you at least dislike him?"

I kissed her again, hoping she would let the matter slide. Her obsession with making me admit that I hated Prakash led to my obsession with being fair. It would be grossly unfair for me to hate a man for marrying her before me.

"Do you?" she prodded.

"I will dislike anyone you want me to dislike." I kissed her. "I will hate anyone you want me to hate." I kissed her again. "And—"

"Even at this age . . . you two." Komal saved me from saying anything more. Her eyes were full of reproach as she came into the kitchen. Anjali and I had been married thirteen years now and Komal couldn't understand our intimacy. Couples were not supposed to be this amorous at our age. It probably boggled her mind that we even had sex . . . with each other.

Anjali tried to withdraw from my embrace, but I held her

tightly. "Yes, even at this age," I said to Komal in a "no non-sense" tone she recognized. This was none of her business. My relationship with my wife was ours alone—no one told us how to live our lives.

I looked down at Anjali and she was trying her best not to laugh by pursing her lips tightly. Komal made a disgruntled sound and left us.

Anjali burst out laughing as soon as Komal was out of earshot, and I joined her, drawing her close to me.

S A N D E E P

When I first met Anjali, I barely noticed her. She slipped past my eyes. If it weren't for my colleague and friend Professor Gopalnath Mishra, who we all called Gopi, I wouldn't have known her at all. He introduced us on the side of a road, on a hot day in July, when you could smell the sweat on human bodies from miles away.

She had the sun in her face and when she looked at me she shaded her eyes with her hand. It had been a chance meeting. We were on our way from the department building to the canteen to get a cup of tea and some university gossip. Gopi knew Anjali well. He had been a friend of the family.

She was working on her master's in education, while Gopi and I taught at the Department of Mathematics and Statistics at the Hyderabad Central University.

We talked aimlessly for a short while and then I suggested we go to the canteen, "before one of us has a sun stroke."

She said she was tired and would like to go back to her hostel. Apparently she was taking some summer classes. I wanted to ask her why she wasn't going back home for the summer, but decided it was none of my business. I had no idea, then, how much of my business everything about Anjali would become.

I was thirty-one, past the social average age of marriage. There was no one to question me. My father died when I was eighteen and my mother passed away when I was twenty-five, just when I was finishing my Ph.D. I spent the next six years building a career and arranging my sister Komal's marriage.

That done, I lost my taste for marriage. Komal's wedding had been a damned negotiation. Her heart was set on marrying a bank officer and Jaydev was a bank officer. He said he would like to marry Komal right after the bride-seeing ceremony. But his parents warned me that their boy was a catch, and as such demanded a high dowry. I was against the idea of perpetuating the despicable custom, but Komal insisted.

"All my friends are married and they all had to give a dowry. Why do you have to start a crusade now? You don't have to take any dowry when you get married, but I want to get married. Now." She wailed for a long time, and finally I gave in.

I sold our parents' house, added my savings to the money I got from the sale, and married Komal off. It was a relief to see her go. She had become a thorn in my side—living with me, nagging me. She was like the wife I never had, and with her gone, I didn't feel like replacing her.

And even if I did want a wife, the path to marriage seemed to be cluttered with too many obstacles.

There were two ways to get married: either your marriage was arranged or you fell in love and got married. I didn't really believe in falling in love—it seemed like it was part of a book or a movie, not real life, and arranged marriage seemed to be a gamble I wasn't ready to risk my life on. I wanted to marry—I didn't want to be celibate and alone for the rest of my life, but I wanted to know the woman before I married her. It didn't seem too much to ask, did it? I just wanted to know the person I was to spend the rest of my life with, before I committed myself to spending the rest of my life with her.

Gopi always told me that was a "charming" idea, but I would have to move out of the country to do that. I had seen friends and others fall in love and get married. The idea of meeting a woman and falling in quasi love with her, knowing her, respecting her before I married her, seemed wise. However, intelligent women were scarce and I couldn't imagine spending the rest of my life with a bubbly little girl who had her heart set on a professor. The girl would have to be incredibly stupid, too, if she wanted to marry a middle-aged professor—our kind didn't make a whole lot of money and I *was* thirty-one. Most young women wanted to marry the wealthy M.B.A. types or the doctors or the army officers. Professors were one of the last resorts for most girls and their parents.

By the time a man reaches my age, people start wondering why he is still single. Maybe he is impotent! Maybe he *is* already married and isn't telling anyone, and so on and so forth. It was a standard question people asked me: it started with "Where is your wife?" and ended with "Why aren't you married?"

Gopi's wife Sarita had tried to marry me off and had given up. Sarita would warn me, "You will die alone, ever thought about that?" and I would tell her that we all die alone.

Gopi and Sarita had an arranged marriage and, for the most part, they seemed content. They too lived on campus and I visited them often. The professors' accommodations were decent. The roof never leaked (well, it did once), but they fixed it before the monsoon ended and the overhead water tank saved us from waking up at four in the morning to fill buckets of water—especially in the summer when water was scarce. To me it was a luxury to have a water tank that collected the water whenever the Hyderabad municipality released it. All my life, I remember waking up at strange hours, filling up every empty utensil we could find at home with water.

The university provided me with a one-bedroom flat—a pigeonhole—because I was a bachelor. Gopi was elevated to a two-bedroom house because of his married status. I spent many nights in Gopi's house, not because it was better than mine, but because Gopi and Sarita were the closest I had to family in Hyderabad.

I had been leading a good life; when I met Anjali—it got better.

I saw her again, two or three weeks later at Gopi and Sarita's house. She had come over for dinner and I realized that Gopi and Sarita were trying to fix us up.

They had it set up well, though they were not subtle about it. Sarita went inside the kitchen and refused Anjali's offer to help. Then she called out to Gopi, who instantly left for the kitchen. They were probably peeking out of the kitchen door, watching the two of us. We both knew what was going on. I was trying to feel outraged but the amusement in Anjali's eyes made me wonder if Gopi and Sarita were off the mark. I had expected she would be demure and eager; instead, she was casual and not at all eager.

"If I'd known, I would have worn my nice *salwar kameez*," she said with mock sweetness, and I laughed.

"And I would have worn something nicer myself," I joined her, looking disparagingly at my worn black nylon pants and white cotton shirt that used to have blue stripes several years ago.

"I am sure your parents wouldn't want Sarita and Gopi to find a husband for you," I said seriously.

What were Gopi and Sarita thinking? Anjali's parents would be extremely upset if they learned of Gopi and Sarita's machinations. I didn't even know if we were from the same caste. Not that it mattered to me, but it could matter to Anjali and her parents.

"My parents wouldn't care," she said, which surprised me.

"They must be very broad-minded."

She made a sound that was halfway between a genuine laugh and hysteria. "They would have a seizure if they knew I was getting married—" She paused gently and then looked into my eyes. "—again."

I slumped into my chair. "Oh, you are married. I think we misunderstood our friends."

She shook her head, biting her lip nervously. "I *was* married."

"I am so sorry. When did he pass away?" I was relieved to

learn she was a widow. For a moment there I thought Gopi, Sarita, and I were making asses of ourselves.

She made a face. "Why is it that everyone thinks that the only way a woman can get rid of her husband is when he dies?"

I was not a chauvinist by a long shot, so for a moment what she said confused me a little. How else could she have been married? And yet . . . no, she wasn't talking about divorce. No one divorced in this country. Divorces happened in movies and with film stars and rich people. Middle-class people didn't divorce. They got married and lived . . . ever after—together.

"You see my parents didn't approve of the divorce," she said almost conversationally. "So they've written me out of the family will."

Her voice, tone, and behavior indicated the divorce had been a simple and normal thing, almost as simple and normal as buying vegetables in the market. Her tone made me feel she was joking, but what she was saying was not a joking matter. So I wondered if she was putting me on.

"You don't believe me, do you?" she asked, noticing my confusion and disbelief.

I was about to say something, probably something stupid because my mind had stopped working rationally, when Sarita came into the living room, flustered. She announced that dinner was ready.

I asked Gopi about it later and he told me that Anjali had divorced her husband two years ago. Gopi didn't know the reasons and he had never tried to find out. She had been distraught after she came back from Bhopal, where she and her husband had lived for less than a year. That was how long the marriage had lasted. Apparently, she didn't have any place to go for the summer, so she stayed at the hostel.

He didn't give too many details, because he didn't know much. For all her vivacity, Anjali seemed to keep to herself. In any case, I yelled at Gopi for pulling the "fix-up" stunt on me and made him promise to never put me in such a situation again. Gopi took it in good humor and so did Sarita. They both agreed, teasingly, that Anjali deserved better.

I had wondered then if Gopi had made a slip of the tongue when he said Anjali had divorced her husband. Women didn't go around divorcing their husbands. Although it was rare, if a divorce did take place it was almost always the man's doing.

I didn't lose any sleep on trying to figure out who was responsible for Anjali and her husband's divorce. I forgot about her for the rest of the summer.

I visited my sister and her husband for a couple of weeks that summer and listened to Komal complain about not having any children. Komal and her husband had both taken fertility tests and the tests clearly rested the blame on Jaydev and his low sperm count. Of course, it had to be a big secret. Jaydev could hardly tell his family and friends that he was not a "real man," as he put it.

So after all the dowry I had given, Komal was not happy with the bank officer she'd had her heart set on marrying. I listened to her complain about her fate in life and I listened to Jaydev complain about his fate in life. They both felt free to complain to me and tell me their sad stories because I was the most "nontraditional" person in the family, as they put it. This meant that I wouldn't be pointing fingers at them anytime soon, which would have been the case if anyone found out that Komal and Jaydev were having serious marital problems.

Komal said her husband wasn't addressing the situation and that everyone in his family was blaming her for not having children. Jaydev said that Komal emasculated him by always talking about his low sperm count. She would make one concoction after another—from recipes dug out of ancient books like the *Kamasutra* to recipes given away for ten *rupees* each by quack *sadhus*—to improve his sperm count. Jaydev was taking some medicines, but they weren't working either. Much of the problem was that Jaydev just didn't feel like having sex anymore because he felt his masculinity had left him when he found out about his low sperm count. Since they were not having sex, there was no chance for a pregnancy.

It was almost four months after the "set-up" dinner at Gopi's that Anjali and I met again. She was talking to a friend outside the auditorium where the students of the Department of Literature were performing a play. As a member of the faculty I had a free ticket, and since I had nothing better to do on a Saturday night I went to see *A Midsummer Night's Dream*.

Our eyes met as we waited to go inside the theater, and before I could turn away and pretend I didn't see her she waved lightly. I waved back uncomfortably. I felt uneasy. After all, Gopi and Sarita had tried to set me up with her. I wondered if she was hopeful because of that.

I noticed that she stood out in a crowd because of her shoulder-length straight hair, her height, and her beautiful face.

I on the other hand was thirty-one years old and looked like the average man on the street. No one would give me a second look—I wasn't that ugly or that handsome. We would make an incongruous pair. For the first time I wondered about her ex-husband. I didn't know his name, but I tried to give him a face, a character, and a personality. I tried to fill the idea of her ex-husband with life, to see who this striking woman had been married to and then divorced from.

She made her way to me and asked me how my summer was. I had no choice but to be polite, though I didn't want to talk to her. She probably had some ideas about me, about herself and me—thanks to Sarita—and I wanted to discourage her.

She realized soon enough that I didn't want to speak with her and left. I should have been relieved, but I wasn't. I felt guilty for being so presumptuous.

I saw a flash of her white *dupatta* as I entered the auditorium, and I don't know what possessed me, but I sat in the empty chair next to her. She didn't notice me, since she was turned the other way, speaking with her friend in a hushed voice.

When the lights went down, without much deliberation or thought, I leaned over and whispered, "I am sorry." The reaction was not what I expected. She squealed and all heads turned to look for the squealer. The curtains went up and the crowd went back to looking at the stage. Anjali and I sat frozen, her squeal still ringing in our ears.

"Sorry again," I whispered, and she was breathing heavily, assuring her companion, who seemed agitated, that everything was all right.

"I didn't expect you to sit with me after . . ." she muttered, looking ahead at the stage.

"I wanted to apologize for that. I think I took too much for granted."

"Like what?"

"Like . . . I thought that Sarita might have given you some ideas . . ."

"Shh," someone said, and we both fell silent.

I blindly looked at the stage for a while, not in the least interested in how Titania and Oberon would make up. I had behaved like an arrogant swine. Did I really think that this wonderful woman would fall all over me?

I couldn't stand it any longer as guilt made me ignore the fact that we were in a theater. When Bottom began to sing, I leaned over again. "I want to apologize. It was very rude of me."

She turned around right then and our noses clashed. She giggled first and I joined her. Someone from the crowd again said, "Shh."

"Out," she whispered, then leaned over to tell her friend something. We stole out of the auditorium like thieves.

"I like *A Midsummer Night's Dream*," she accused me with a broad smile as soon as we were outside.

"I am sorry," I said with a broad smile. "I think I have apologized enough, don't you?"

She seemed to think it over, her arms folded against her chest. "Maybe *chai* will ease the pain of missing the play and soothe hurt feelings."

"*Chai?*"

"Yes," she said, then sighed. "I am not trying to wrangle a

marriage out of my stay here at the university. I am just going to get my master's and leave."

"Who talked about marriage?" I asked, feigning ignorance.

"You yelled at Gopi for trying to set us up," she said in an accusatory tone.

"Well . . . it was stupid of him and Sarita."

"I agree," she said, and I wished she had disagreed with me. So began an unusual friendship.

Yes, we were friends. I think we became lovers and got married because we were friends. We met each other regularly after that night. Sometimes she would wait for me to show up at the canteen or the library, or I would meet her after one of her classes.

Gopi and Sarita gave each other sly glances when the four of us were together, while Anjali and I tried to convince them that we were just friends. A novelty, certainly. I hadn't seen too many single men being "just friends" with a woman. But it was true in our case.

I discovered I was in love almost a year after the night we missed watching *A Midsummer Night's Dream*.

It was the end of her master's and she was in my flat studying for finals, since the dorms were crowded and noisy despite the need for silence.

Her breath was labored and each time she inhaled she made a hissing sound. She was studying on my dining/study table in the living room. I was trying to cook a decent meal for us in the adjoining kitchen.

I asked her if anything was wrong and she shook her head, but when she clutched at her chest trying to breathe, I started to panic. I wanted to call an ambulance, get her into an emergency room. And then her eyes bulged out and she fell to the floor. Needless to say by then I was insane with panic.

She managed to grab her bag that was lying by the feet of the chair she had been sitting on and yanked out an inhaler from inside it.

When she could breathe again, she told me she had asthma and how she had gotten it. I listened intently, in rapture that she had survived one of the worst chemical catastrophes of the century. I had read about the Bhopal gas tragedy, and they still talked about it on the news two years after the fact. Analysts had likened it to the atomic bomb disasters in Japan. And Anjali had been there that night, breathing the poisonous gas. And she was here now with me, struggling to breathe.

I couldn't get a handle on it.

"What about your ex-husband?" I asked her. "Was he affected, too?"

She shook her head. "No, the wind blew in the other direction."

Even though the Union Carbide factory was only four kilometers from the EME Center where her husband was, the wind was blowing toward Bhopal City, away from the EME Center, and that had saved her husband's life. She also told me that the night of the gas tragedy he forgot to pick her up at the railway station.

"If only he had come when my train got there," she said, "I would've been saved. . . . Well, I was saved, I didn't die."

"Is this why you divorced him?" I wasn't curious or prying by nature, but in my mind her ex-husband had taken a life of his own.

"No. I left him because he cheated on me," she said simply, and her tone indicated the end of that conversation.

After that she didn't talk about him much. The divorce was still in the recent past and she mentioned him only once in a while. Prakash was her ex-husband, but she always said that she didn't think of him like that. They had been married for less than a year and the marriage itself had seemed like an experiment or a test to her. She may have failed the test, but she was not going to give up on life because of it.

Anjali's asthma attack made me take stock of things. For an instant I had thought she would die and that had all but crippled me. It was a simple thing. Firecrackers didn't go off and the earth didn't move, but almost like a breeze caressing me, I realized that I was in love with Anjali. It was a pleasant thought and a comforting one. She was one of my closest friends. I enjoyed her company. She was playful, smart, strong, and independent. She wasn't the type of woman who would sit at home and keep house for her husband; she would go out and stand shoulder to shoulder with men.

She would be a partner and a wife; she would be a friend and a lover. I knew I wanted to marry her and I asked her as soon as her finals were over.

The students were celebrating the last day of their master's all over the university campus. Some of the students were coming back to do their M.Phil. and some wanted to pursue a Ph.D. I knew about Anjali's plans; she wanted to become a schoolteacher. She didn't want to live in Hyderabad. She wanted to live in a quiet, small place, "A place where the air is fresh and hills are kissed by rolling fog."

I was glad I met Anjali at Hyderabad Central University.

In another university, I would have lost my job and she would have been suspended for fraternizing with a professor. Here things were slightly different—more open. That was one of the reasons why I had taken up the job there. My class syllabus was flexible, and I could take a class to the canteen if my students were hungry. I could sit outside under the trees and teach my students, or go on a hike during class. I had free rein in teaching my students and I enjoyed that. My personal life was not judged by anyone and that was an added bonus. It was the broad-mindedness of the university that allowed Anjali and me to have a healthy friendship instead of a scandalous affair.

I didn't know how to propose. I had no idea what to say to Anjali. She was chatting with one of her friends as we sat around a bonfire burning away the past year. Anjali turned to me and smiled, while I nervously fidgeted with words in my mind.

"I am going to miss you," I said, and she smiled again, that dazzling smile.

"Why, Professor, one would think we are never going to see each other again," she mocked with amusement.

"Not as often, at least."

"We can meet during summer vacations, or . . . I don't know, make an effort to meet, if we want to."

"Or we could get married," I blurted out.

She looked like I had slammed a fist into her solar plexus. She swallowed visibly. "I thought I heard you say that we should get married."

I nodded blindly.

She covered her face with her hands for a moment and then raised her head to look at me. Her eyes widened and she all but stopped breathing again. I hoped she was not going to have another asthma attack. I didn't think my ego would be able to handle that.

"You want to get married?" she asked.

"Yes . . . to you."

"Why?"

"Because . . ." My mind raced to find answers, to find convincing arguments, but all I could say was, "Because I am in love with you."

The confusion on her face fell and she smiled.

A month later, we got married in the Hyderabad registrar's office, with a smug Gopi and Sarita as our witnesses. It was the best wedding I had ever attended. This one was small, didn't have too many unnecessary guests, just Gopi and Sarita; it was extremely inexpensive (especially compared to the farce my sister went through); and best of all I was marrying a woman I was deeply in love with.

I had called my sister before the wedding to tell her about Anjali and had promised her that we would visit them in Delhi soon. Komal was disappointed that there was not going to be a "real" wedding, and that was the first thing about Anjali she didn't like. Once she met Anjali, there were other things she didn't like about her, so we never told her about Anjali's previous life as an army officer's wife.

Anjali and I threw a party in the university auditorium a day after the wedding, inviting all our friends. Anjali had invited her parents, but they never showed up.

I was dazed—it had happened. I had fallen in love and I had married.

But I couldn't help wondering how Anjali felt. She was

getting married without her family, without the usual trappings of a large wedding. It was a "sign here, please" kind of wedding, miles apart from her first one where all the ceremonies had been held and no expenses had been spared.

Again, I wondered about Prakash. Had he been this incandescently happy when he had married my Anjali?

P R A K A S H

"I saw her at the market today," Indu told me as soon as she came home. "She was with her husband—simple-looking man. I think they are very happy."

I shrugged as if it didn't matter to me.

Our cook took the vegetables from Indu and she sat down on the sofa. She sprawled on it, her body meshing with the velvet fabric, yet she managed to look alert and sharp. It was a lazy posture, but Indu never looked lazy. She looked ladylike, no, queenlike.

"I can't imagine why you divorced her," Indu said. She simply couldn't waste such a perfect opportunity to bring up the past and my failures.

Maybe I should have told the truth to Indu from the start, that Anju had divorced me. But pride had come in the way. I didn't want Indu to know that I was divorced because I had committed adultery.

"What is that supposed to mean?" I demanded.

Indu smoothed the pleats of her sari and smiled. She looked so smug: as if she knew all my secrets, as if she knew what made me tick, as if she knew me. Sometimes I wanted to tell her about what had happened with Anju, just so that I could wipe that smug all-knowing look off her face. Unwittingly I had left Anju to die the night of the Bhopal gas tragedy—that was my terrible secret. And sometimes I wanted to tell Indu about it. To show her that she didn't know everything about me and that I had done far worse things than divorcing a wife.

"Oh, just that she seems your type," she said, with a nonchalance I could barely stand. "She must've been a good-looking woman. Now . . . she needs a serious makeover, but she is quite a looker."

I gritted my teeth against saying anything. Why did Anju have to live here? It was easier when Indu spoke about my ex-wife when she couldn't picture her. Now Indu had seen her, heard her voice, spoken to her, and she punished me for that. For having an ex-wife, for having an ex-wife she had had to meet.

Indu was a leftenant general's daughter, and knew no world outside the army. It was always a given that she would marry an army officer. I just happened to be at the right place at the right time. After the divorce I had been posted out of Bhopal to Baroda, where Indu's father was commanding the EME College.

While I was reeling with shock from my divorce, Indu had been reeling me in as her husband. She hadn't known about my divorce in the beginning, when we first started seeing each other. When I told her about Anju, I thought she would leave me, but she didn't. She told me she was in love with me and it didn't matter that there had been a woman in the past.

"She seems the doormat, Prakash," Indu said, looking into my eyes, trying to see how I was reacting to the knowledge in hers. "Perfect for you. Wouldn't you have been happier with a smitten doormat than with me?"

Why did she always have to test the limits of my patience? Sometimes I thought about leaving Indu, but divorcing her would ruin my career in the army. When Anju and I divorced, we'd been married less than a year and everything was forgotten and forgiven by the army. I had been a captain then; now I was a brigadier. Things were different. Indu was different. She wouldn't disappear into the night the way Anju had. Indu would stand up and tell the world that I was at fault, and my chances of promotion would be sealed within the papers of my second divorce.

I could become the leftenant general of the EME Corps. Age was on my side and my records were impeccable. And I had just secured a prestigious post at the EME Staff College, here at Wellington. I was set to succeed, to command the entire EME Corps, and that to me was more important than finding peace without Indu. She knew that. She knew that her father could and would use his influence when the time came for me to become leftenant general. We both had that one common goal—so we smiled together at parties and came back home to claw at each other. If Indu had been submissive, like so many army officers' wives were, my life would have been easier. But Indu was not docile and no matter how I tried I couldn't bend her to my will.

"You think she is more beautiful than me?" she asked

suddenly, and I was off balance again. But I had lived with her for thirteen years now; I knew her just as well as she thought she knew me.

"I divorced her, remember." I perpetuated the lie. "What is this about, Indu?" I changed my tone to soothe her, to gain her trust again, as she sat there looking at me with accusing eyes. She drove me to madness sometimes with her ability to push all my right buttons.

It was during these times that I wished Anju had never divorced me. When things were terrible with Indu, I blamed Anju for my life. If she had stayed, if she had given us another chance, I wouldn't be married to Indu. Other times when things were good, I was glad that Anju had left, so that I had the chance to build a new and better life with Indu. I felt like a yo-yo, changing positions as my circumstances changed. My relationship with Indu had never been this bad before, but Indu had never met Anju before. Now that she had, some bizarre sort of anger was eating her up. She always had her nails sheathed. Now they were unsheathed and she was clawing at my soul.

"She seemed very happy with her simple husband and she probably has a simple life," Indu spoke suddenly, and I sat down next to her. Her tone was not as sharp as before and that meant she was not going to throw something at me.

"She is not part of our life," I soothed.

Indu laughed mirthlessly. "You were married to her once. She will always be part of our life."

I ran my hands through my hair impatiently. "Why do you have to bring her up? She has moved on, I have moved on, so why the hell can't you?"

Anger was usually not a good approach with Indu when

she was in one of her intractable moods as she was now. My anger fed her anger and she became downright hostile. On the other hand, when I went from angry to caring, I got better results.

"She is in my past, Indu," I said softly, sitting down next to her and taking her hand in mine. "And we had an arranged marriage. You know how those work? We barely spoke to each other before we were married."

"But you did after," she pointed out, though the fight and taunt had left her voice. "All marriages work somehow. I mean . . . I don't know anyone who is divorced, except you."

I stroked her cheek gently. I abhorred the situation we were in. We were caught up in a game. We wore masks all the time. During parties, during sex, when we were with our children— all the time we wore the damned masks. We had been wearing masks for so long, our real faces were gone. We had expressions for occasions, moods, and points in life.

"I am sorry that I didn't meet you a year before I did," I said, putting on a charming smile, which had lured many a woman to my bed in the past. "If I had, I would have married you and Anju would be—"

"Why do you call her Anju? Her name is Anjali."

I bit my lip. I was walking on eggshells with Indu. It wasn't a slip of the tongue. Anjali was Anju to me.

"I love you, Indu." I leaned down and slowly let my lips brush against hers. Before I could deepen the kiss she pulled away.

"No," she said, pushing me away. "I just saw her and a wife doesn't like to be seduced when she is thinking of how her husband lay naked with another woman."

I didn't stop her when she walked out of the drawing room. If only Anju hadn't divorced me, I wouldn't be in the mess I was in today. If she had only stayed.

Sweet, beautiful, sexy, intelligent Anju! Now, much of the beauty and sexiness was gone. Yet there was something within her that hadn't been there before. It was her eyes, I remembered. Her eyes were bright now. As if she had found her purpose and her meaning. When we had been married she'd had stars in her eyes, now she had confidence and maturity.

When I first saw Anju, I'd wondered if I should run as fast as I could, or stay and deal with it. In Udhampur, from where I had been posted out of (rather, thrown out of, because of a certain delicate matter), Colonel Chaudhary's gorgeous wife had not been as discreet as I had hoped and certain key people in the command had learnt about our affair. It soon became an open secret and the silent accusations were deafening. The commanding officer of the unit, Brigadier Joshi, called me into his office, handed me my transfer papers, and advised me to get married. He gave me a month off to find a wife and then report for duty in Bhopal, where he hoped I would be a good husband and avoid scandals.

I was twenty-five, cocky, and ready to jump into bed with anything gorgeous—unmarried or single. I preferred experience and kept away from the innocent-looking ones. The innocent ones were dangerous—some of them were beautiful and beckoning and dangerous because they could trap me into marriage. As soon as I saw Anju, I knew she was the innocent type and I had wanted to run.

But I knew I had to get married even though I didn't want to. I wanted to play the field a little more, as I told my father. His advice was simple: get married and still play the field. But I didn't want to play the field with a wife waiting at home in bed for me. I didn't want a wife waiting at home in bed for me at all.

However, I knew that if I didn't get married, things would get ugly for me. The EME Corps was a small place and word traveled fast.

When Divya Auntie introduced me to Anju, she was as green as I thought she would be and as smitten as I hoped she wouldn't be. She seemed to be in awe of everything army. After our marriage, she had been excited when she first saw me in uniform and she had been excited when we got an orderly to do things at home. The only time she was unexcited was in bed. I didn't like having sex with her and thankfully she didn't want to have sex with me. I didn't know what to do with her. She was like an appendage that had grown out of my life, and I couldn't adjust to her. Our first night had been a disaster because I really had not wanted to be there to consummate a marriage I didn't want. I didn't want to indulge in foreplay. I was being forced into marriage and I hated Anju for being the one I had to marry. It was not Anju's fault; I would have hated any woman in her place.

Once in Bhopal, it took me less than a week to realize that my beautiful wife could charm the pants off anyone. I introduced her to Colonel Shukla, my new commanding officer in Bhopal, and he was impressed with her. He nudged and winked and told me that I had a wonderful and beautiful wife. A good wife was an asset in the army. She could be the perfect hostess and she could kiss ass and say the right things and upset no one. I couldn't have asked for more. As long as she kept my commanding officer's wife charmed, there was little chance my yearly work reports would be less than stellar. So, I learned to live with her, even though I didn't enjoy it.

I was selfish then—and maybe I haven't changed much—but now I could see who I was. That was hard to do when I was twenty-five. I was a good army officer with the perfect official record and there was no shortage of women for me.

We came to Bhopal in mid-May, just a week after the wedding. We'd had a honeymoon of sorts in Goa, but neither of us had much fun. I treated her badly, for the first month at least. But she persevered and tried to please me, which enraged me even more. But things started to change after the first month. I got used to her. When I came home, she was there with a beaming smile and a cup of tea. She always had the best meals ready whenever I felt like one and she made an absolutely stunning hostess. I invited other officers over and showed the hell off with the wife I didn't want.

I was young and stupid. If I had known any better, I would have treated her like a princess and taken care of her as if she were precious.

Anju had been a delight I had failed to notice. And now she was lost to me. She was married to another man, who, according to Indu, seemed to keep her happy.

I was suddenly obsessed with seeing her with her husband and seeing her . . . didn't she say she had a son? Yes, she had. She had a child. A child with another man.

Indu and I had two children. A daughter and a son. My life with Indu was perfect on paper. We were prosperous, had a son and a daughter, and I was going to be leftenant general someday soon.

Until I saw Anju again, I had convinced myself that she left me because she hadn't wanted to make the marriage work. Now that I had seen her, the guilt was back. I knew that I hadn't let the marriage even begin. In my mind she had gone from being a safety net for my embarrassing affair with Mrs. Chaudhary, to an impediment, and finally to a nonentity.

A N J A L I

Sandeep continued to be evasive about Prakash and I finally gave up. I wanted to tell him why Prakash's wife, Indu, affected me. I corrected myself instantly—she was Prakash's Indu. To me she was Indira.

After Prakash and I divorced, I started clearly spelling out my "correct" name to people. Everyone started calling me Anjali; no one shortened it to Anju. Some had tried and I had fought against it. I'd argue that my parents had given me a perfectly reasonable name, that it didn't need to be shortened. People backed away after that, wondering if I was some sort of a nut who was hung up on names.

I took Amar for his weekly check-up on Thursdays because my classes ended early that day. The school administration cut me slack because they knew about Amar. They didn't mind if I left early on some days or had to take an extra sick day because

Amar was not feeling well. I didn't take advantage of it, just in case someone would object and the small perks I did have would be snatched away. Worse, I could lose my job, and my job helped pay Amar's medical bills.

Amar squirmed in the auto rickshaw and I tried to make him more comfortable. "Why are the roads always so bumpy?" he complained. "Does no one ever fix them?"

I gave him a wry look. "What do you think?"

"Right." He nodded, and we laughed together.

He could laugh, I thought, as my heart split apart. He could still laugh, while most grown-ups would have given up.

"Do I still have to take those shots?" he asked, as he did every week when we went to the doctor, and I nodded.

"Can I just take the pills in the morning and not take the shots?" he asked. "The shots make me sick."

"I know," I said, and patted his hand. "But we need to find out if they work."

Amar was on a strict regimen of corticosteroid pills every day. A month ago his doctor suggested that we try some new corticosteroid shots and see if there would be a difference.

"Sometimes . . . ," he looked out of the auto instead of at me, "I wish it would all end. I mean, you and Daddy spend so much money—"

"Money is not something you should think about," I interrupted him sternly. "You are my precious baby and nothing bad is ever going to happen to you. So don't worry about anything and concentrate on getting better. Okay?"

He smiled shakily. "Something bad has already happened to me, Mummy. I am getting more and more tired and . . ."

I didn't want to hear it. I didn't want him to give up. Not now, when he had beaten the odds for twelve years.

"You just worry about getting better." My voice was shaky. I never cried in front of him. It was our rule. Sandeep and I wanted to smile when we were with Amar. There would be no fighting, no yelling, and no screaming in front of our son. He would see the world around him as a happy place, not a devastating one.

Amar patted my hand to comfort me and I choked on tears. This was not living—this was the purest kind of hell. My sick baby had to comfort me.

Amar's doctor repeated what Amar had said earlier. Amar was getting weaker and his lungs were not getting any better.

"The inflammation is not going down and the scar tissue is spreading in his lungs," Doctor Anand Raman said. "I wish I could say something else. But considering how things were, Amar is very lucky."

Lucky?

"You are lucky to be alive, Anjali," he said, when he saw the anger in my eyes.

We'd had this discussion several times. I would always vent that no one had bothered to tell me that the Bhopal gas tragedy had left its mark on my womb. I wish someone had told me that having a child would be dangerous to the child, that any child I had would be affected by that fateful night in Bhopal when so many lost their lives and so many were left wounded forever.

Amar got his shots and I shelled out over six hundred *rupees* for his medication for the week and the doctor's visit. All his pills went into a red wooden box that sat on his bedside table. On the box, Amar had himself painted the words *Amar's Medicine*. He had painted the box five years ago, when he was seven, right after his heart surgery, which we had hoped would cure him. He had told me, "When I stop using the box, I will still keep it." Then, he had had hope that someday the box would be empty and he would be a normal child. Now, five years later as his condition deteriorated, he seemed to be changing his mind about life and death.

Komal was sitting in front of the television when Amar and I got home. She looked up at us but didn't say anything, and I wondered once again why she hated me so much. Our relationship from the beginning had been tenuous, now it was worse. Familiarity was breeding contempt, just as the old cliché promised.

Amar sat down on the sofa next to Komal, tired after being out and tired from the shots that kept him breathing.

"We are having Gopi and Sarita for dinner," I told Komal. She nodded without looking at me.

Gopi and Sarita were coming with their two children, Ajay and Shalini. Two healthy, adorable children. They were our closest friends, had been with us through the worst and the best of times, yet I was envious of their children. They went to school and didn't get tired after walking for five minutes.

As I headed for the kitchen, Komal made a sound, something in between a curse and a prayer.

I sighed. "Can you come into the kitchen with me, Komal?"

Once in the kitchen, I decided to stop beating around the bush. "What have I done now?" I asked flatly.

Komal looked away, not saying anything.

"Oh come on, if you don't tell me, how am I supposed to know?" I insisted.

She sniffled and I thought it was a mistake to have asked her at all. The woman was being melodramatic, while I had to cook for guests.

"Today is his . . . death anniversary," she said, and sniffled some more. "No one has done anything. I wanted to go to the temple, but Sandeep is not here to take me and I can't walk to the temple, my knee is bothering me again."

"Why didn't you tell us?" I asked. It was an important day for her. I had other problems to deal with and couldn't keep track of the days someone died on.

"You should know. My own brother doesn't remember. I have no family." She started sobbing.

I patted her shoulder awkwardly, unsure of how to comfort her. I couldn't imagine life without Sandeep—and suddenly I felt a pang of guilt for treating Komal the way I did. She was a widow, a pariah in society. She was going to live like this for the rest of her life. Nothing was going to change. She was forever going to be a burden to someone.

In some ways she was in the same position I was in when I divorced Prakash, though my situation had been worse. Society forgave widows for their husbands' deaths, but they didn't forgive women like me, who let their husbands go on purpose.

My parents had gone berserk and so had Prakash. No one could believe I was divorcing him. Prakash had even refused to give me a divorce and had relented only when I told him I would start naming names of women he had been with to make a case for divorce on the basis of adultery. After that, he hadn't protested much and I had gotten what I wanted, freedom from my husband.

Komal, on the other hand, had not wanted to be free of her husband. She had not wanted him to be run over by a city bus. She was alone in the world. She didn't have children, her husband was dead, and she was stuck with us.

"Would you like to go to the temple now?" I asked patiently. "Sandeep should be home soon and he can take you."

Komal looked at me with something like surprise in her eyes. I didn't like seeing that. Did I really come across as some bitch who wouldn't let her widowed sister-in-law go to a temple on her husband's death anniversary? I didn't even tell her what to do or what not to do. Her life was hers, but I knew she couldn't understand that she was free to do what she wanted. How could she? She had listened to her father, then her husband, and now she felt she needed to listen to Sandeep because he paid the bills. I felt sorry for her, but I knew she wouldn't have it any other way. Komal was raised, just the way I was, to obey the men in her life.

"He is here? In Ooty?" Sarita squealed.

I made a hissing sound to silence her. "Yes, and he had the nerve to come to school to talk to me."

We were in the kitchen, putting the finishing touches on our dinner. Sandeep and Gopi were on the veranda with Komal, and Amar was playing with Sarita's children.

Sarita's oldest, Ajay, was Amar's age and Shalini was a couple of years younger. Ajay and Shalini understood that Amar was sick and came by whenever they could to keep the "sick boy" company. I was glad they did, but it felt like charity, nevertheless.

"I also met his wife," I told Sarita. It was a pleasure to gossip with someone. I was, after all, a woman and I had to talk about what was going on in my life. Sandeep knew all of it, so there was no point in telling him.

"What was she like?"

"Pretty, pretty."

"Not prettier than you," Sarita claimed, and I laughed.

"I don't want him, Sarita," I told her, as I sprinkled chopped coriander on the *dum aloo*.

"I know, but you know what I am trying to say," she said.

"I know," I said, and sighed. "Can we talk about something else?"

"How was the doctor's appointment? Any improvement?" Sarita asked.

I shook my head. "No, the lung inflammation is not getting any better and his heart is the same. To make it worse, the scar tissue has started to spread in his lungs."

"If only the heart operation had worked. He is such a smart boy," Sarita said.

Tears filled my eyes. "Yes, and today he said that sometimes he wanted it all to be over. The corticosteroids shot makes him sick and . . . there is nothing I can do to make it better."

"Ice cream," Sarita said firmly. "Children always feel better if you give them ice cream. I have some *pista kulfi* at home; Gopi will get it right away."

I tried to stop her, but what was the point? Sarita never listened to anyone.

The *kulfi* did help. Amar was grinning from ear to ear as he ate the homemade pistachio ice cream, despite the cold weather.

After dinner, Gopi dropped off his kids and put them to bed and came right back. The four of us did that often. We sat and talked late into the night. Komal stayed with us for a while and then usually left.

And it was like the old times again. The four of us, together, alone.

"I know you don't want to talk about this," Gopi began, and I was on alert. "But you should join this class action lawsuit against Union Carbide."

"And then what?" I questioned.

"You might get a good settlement."

"And then?"

Gopi exhaled loudly. "And then . . . you will have money, which will help Amar . . ."

"You think lack of money has stopped us in any way?" I demanded, and Sandeep put a restraining hand over my shoulder.

"I can sue Union Carbide, but I can't get my baby to walk and be normal," I said, trying not to yell at Gopi. "No amount of money is going to change that."

Sarita was on her husband's side on this one. "But the money will help. You could stay at home with Amar."

"I don't want their money," I said harshly. "What happened, happened. Things happen. I am not going to get into a court trial that could last for god knows how many years, while my son is struggling to live."

Gopi looked thoughtful. "I just thought it might be worth your while. It will make the finances real smooth. A group of people are suing Union Carbide again, but this time it is in the United States . . . so chances are better."

Sandeep shook his head. "It's been over a decade and people are still trying to sue instead of getting on with their lives."

"Oh, you know what I heard? Remember Bhaskar?" Sarita changed the topic as she always did when discussions went awry. "He was a professor in the English Lit department." We all nodded as memory slithered in. "Well, he wrote a movie screenplay that Kamal Hassan bought for . . . lots of money."

The evening drifted away, as we wandered from the topic of the Bhopal gas tragedy to movies to the current political climate to Pakistan.

As we talked about Pakistan, the border dispute, and the Indian army, Sarita took the opportunity to open up the discussion to include an army officer, Prakash.

"Have you met him?" Sarita asked Sandeep.

"Whom?" Gopi questioned.

"Prakash?" Sandeep asked.

"No. Why?"

I closed my eyes. Damn Sarita, couldn't she for once keep her mouth shut?

"Her ex-husband showed up at her school," Sarita told Gopi, and I winced. "To apologize! Sometimes I think you should've bludgeoned him to death. He is the reason for all this. That man . . ."

"Can we not talk about this?" I implored, and Sarita glared at me.

"Why not? Is it taboo?" she demanded.

"No," Sandeep said gently. "It just makes Anjali uncomfortable."

And it did. God, how it did!

I couldn't sleep that night. Sarita and Gopi hated Prakash and they didn't even know him. Sandeep maintained his indifference, and I didn't know how to feel about the man I had once been married to. The man I had lived with for almost a year.

It was so many years ago, yet I seemed to be caught in some time warp where Prakash existed. It was like history repeating itself. Prakash was here again, and once again I wasn't sure what I felt for him.

✸ TWELVE

A N J A L I

I discovered early on in my first marriage that being an army officer's wife was not just fun and games. It was sometimes very boring and sometimes very stressful. It would have been worthwhile if Prakash behaved more like a normal man instead of a homicidal bull caught in a trap.

I knew how he felt about being married. I had found out on our dismal honeymoon. He had told me that he liked me, but he was not sure marrying me had been such a good idea. I was shocked. This was not what I was supposed to hear on my honeymoon. My army officer husband was not the loving, caring man I had thought he would be. So just like in the Hindi movies where the wife has to work at gaining her husband's love, I started working at it.

It was the small things. The cardamom *chai* in the evening when he came back from work, the delicious breakfasts, and the perfect parties—I did everything I could. And finally I think he stopped disliking the idea of marriage. I was an asset and for a while I convinced myself that he even loved me. But in an arranged marriage where love is not important—it is actually a guarantee. The husband will love the wife in some shape or form and the wife will love her husband because he provides for her.

I loved Prakash because he was my husband and because he took care of me financially and because he was what I'd wanted so much. I loved him because not loving him would mean I had been foolish to believe he was the perfect man.

Life in the army was a series of parties, just as I had imagined it would be. The parties were boring—I had not counted on that. Prakash kept to himself, and our marriage was just like the many I had seen growing up. We were strangers living in the same house. We talked once in a while, but it was superficial conversations that gave us something to do besides chew our food at the dining table. We watched television the nights we didn't go out and he always went to bed before I did.

It started to get to me. I was sitting at home all day long with nothing better to do. I cooked and I cleaned and I did the laundry—but I was always bored. I started going to the library and picking up romance novels to fill the time, and it was on one of my trips that I met Harjot Dhaliwal.

Harjot was eighteen, in medical college, and was back home for the summer vacation. She was studying to be a doctor and she was everything I used to not like in a woman. She was intelligent, well educated, and wanted to be independent. She didn't want to get married anytime soon because she wanted to build a career.

We met at the EME Center library where she was going through magazines and I was piling up Mills & Boon romance novels in a plastic bag. She looked at the title of a book I was holding and whistled softly. *"Prisoner of Passion?"*

I laughed when I heard the title read aloud. The books were silly, but they made the time pass. They gave me something to do when Prakash went to sleep and I couldn't. They gave me a fantasy world to walk into. The hero was always cruel and insensitive to the heroine in the beginning, and in the end he was nice to her and in love with her. I had the cruel and insensitive hero; I was waiting for him to become nice and fall in love with me.

"You are Colonel Singh's daughter," I said, stuffing the book back into the shelf.

"You don't have to put it back because of me," Harjot said.

I straightened and smiled sheepishly. "Well, I've already read it."

"You live down the road, right under Major Malhotra's house," she said. "Malhotra Auntie and Mummy are very good friends," she added.

I nodded, not knowing what to say. She was only three years younger than me, but I felt much older. I was a married woman and, in the hierarchical system of society, that made me much older than the years warranted.

"How are you enjoying your summer holidays?" I asked.

"I am bored."

That was exactly how I was feeling, so I invited her over for tea. And that became a ritual.

She came over at around ten every morning and spent the day with me. Prakash came home for lunch sometimes and Harjot stayed, and she noticed how things were between us.

The first time she broached the subject, I wanted to get defensive, but I had no other friends in Bhopal and I was dying to tell someone what I was going through.

"I think he didn't want to marry me," I said. "I don't know why he did. No one forced him to."

I later found out that Harjot had known all about Prakash's problem with women. Apparently several people in the EME Center knew and they all hoped that a beautiful wife like me would keep the good-looking and promising captain from straying.

"Why don't you do a postgraduate?" Harjot suggested.

"But what will I do with it?" I didn't want to go back to college; I had just gotten out of there. "I mean, what job can I hold as an army officer's wife with all that moving?"

"You could be a teacher," Harjot said. "Come on, you could teach in the army schools and there will be one everywhere Prakash gets posted. It could be really nice for you."

"But I don't want to work. I want to be a wife and a mother," I protested.

"You can be a wife and a mother and have a job."

I couldn't believe it then. My mother had always been home, and that had been nice for my younger brother and me. Even though Sanjay was in college and I was married, I liked the idea that my mother was at home. I could visit anytime I wanted to without worrying about her not being available.

"I think it is expecting too much from life to work and be a wife and a mother," I said. "I mean, you will have to stop being a doctor when you have a baby."

Harjot gave me a look reserved for the stupid. "And why would I do that?"

"How can you take care of your baby and work? Babies need their mothers," I said simply.

Needless to say, Harjot was not like me. She wanted equal rights and said that women had to believe in themselves before society would change. I told her that I didn't want society to change. I liked the way things were. I liked the idea of having a husband take care of me while I made a home for him and his children. I didn't want to enter the crazy working world.

The summer ended and Harjot went back to college. By then I had made more friends through her. Mrs. Dhaliwal played rummy with some other wives and I was invited to the card games. It was a lot of fun. There was Mrs. Malhotra who always complained when she lost money, there was Mrs. Khatre who was never on time and made the worst *samosas*, which she insisted were perfect, and there were a few more wives who like me were trying to find a way to pass the time. We spent our afternoons playing cards, or just gossiping about this and that.

Life was not boring anymore. I started paying less attention to Prakash, though he didn't seem to notice. He didn't complain about having toast and jam for breakfast instead of the stuffed *parathas* I used to make, and neither did he complain when I sometimes heated leftover *dal* and curry for dinner. Our life continued as it had before, with us barely talking to each other or spending time together. Earlier I had made the effort to cook what he liked in order to please him; now I had stopped doing that.

We were comfortably apart and, unlike before, I didn't really care anymore.

That changed.

It was in August and a big party was thrown to welcome a visiting brigadier general of the EME Corps. That was where I met Major Vijay Reddy, who had come with the brigadier general. We instantly started talking because he was also from Hyderabad. His parents even lived in Begumpet, just a few blocks from where my parents lived, and his younger sister had gone to the same college as I had.

He was charming and I was charmed. After being neglected by my husband, this attentive man made me feel feminine and attractive. He noticed me, which was more than Prakash seemed to do. We had been married for over three months now and we had never really talked to each other. We were unlike the newly married couples I had known. We had had sex just a few times and we had never gone out together to the city for dinner or someplace else, just the two of us getting to know each other. In the darkness of my current life, Vijay was a perfect and irresistible diversion.

He spent the entire evening with me. The first spark of attraction was ignited that night, though I wouldn't admit it— I was a married woman and married women did not find other men attractive. It was a cardinal rule, which I was fully prepared to follow. But Vijay was tempting and, after all, I was just speaking with him, I rationalized. Just talking to a man didn't mean anything.

I didn't think anyone noticed me with Major Reddy. After all, wives talked to other officers all the time. And indeed, no one noticed, no one except Prakash.

When we got home, I was floating. Vijay had told me I was beautiful and how lucky Prakash was. It was innocuous flirting and I had smiled and laughed with him. What else could I do, when my own husband wore a permanent frown on his face?

"What were you and that Reddy fellow talking about?" Prakash asked, as I unraveled my sari in our bedroom.

I shrugged and didn't answer.

"Well?"

I started to fold the sari and wondered what I could tell him. Vijay and I hadn't really talked about anything tangible, it was just chatting.

"Hyderabad," I finally answered.

"Why such a long time to answer me?"

"What?"

"What?" Prakash yelled. "You were sitting close to him and laughing. It was disgusting. You are my wife, not some ten-*rupee* whore."

For a moment I couldn't believe he had said that. "How dare you call me a whore?" I turned to face him. My eyes glistened with angry tears. This was not happening to me—decent middle-class women were not accused by their husbands of being whores because they had spoken to another man. I was attracted to Vijay, but Prakash had no way of knowing that.

"I dare to call you a whore because you behaved like one," he accused. "Other women might do this kind of thing and get away with it, but my wife will not."

"And other men might doubt their wives, but my husband will not," I retorted forcefully. "I have done nothing, nothing at all to make you say these things. Why would you even think it? I can't talk to anyone else? Is that it?"

"You were *talking* to him?" he said sarcastically. "Is that what they are calling it these days?"

"I don't know what it is that you are talking about. How about when you sit and *talk* with those girls? Priyanka Mallik and you seemed to be extra friendly with each other last Saturday at the *Tambola* party." I didn't really think he was doing anything but talking with Priyanka Mallik, but I wanted to hit back at him.

His face turned red. His hands, which had been unbuckling his belt, stopped, and I took three steps back. I had seen this in the movies and I would be damned if my husband would hit me. That wasn't going to happen, I vowed.

His hands fell from the belt and he sat down on the bed wearily. "What are we doing to ourselves, Anju?" he said, his voice hoarse, traumatized.

My relief was obvious. "I don't know," I confessed, and sat down next to him. This was my husband and I loved him. I put my hand on his shoulder to soothe him.

Prakash sighed and took my hand in his. "I am sorry. I don't know . . . I was jealous seeing you with Reddy."

"I am your wife," I said, even though I was flattered that he was jealous.

"And I am a terrible husband. Right?"

"No," I lied.

"Really?"

"Yes."

He kissed me then, warmly, gently. It was like a kiss from a romance novel. With that kiss our marriage finally entered a tentative honeymoon stage.

He spent the evenings with me and we went to the movies they showed in the EME Center Open Air Theatre on

Wednesdays and Fridays. We spent more time together and he even took me to the city to shop for clothes and jewelry.

Bhopal was about ten kilometers from Bairagarh, where the EME Center was, and we would go away on a Sunday morning and come back late in the night. Prakash even found a restaurant where they served good South Indian food. Ethnically I was North Indian, but I was raised in South India and loved South Indian cuisine. Prakash thought it was too bland, but he came with me and I convinced myself that he did so because he loved me.

I thought that because he was being so warm and gentle, our sex would also take a 180-degree turn. That didn't happen. We were both still uncomfortable. To me it was new. I was shy and scared. I didn't know what his problem was. And I didn't care. I was glad he was having sex with me, because that meant he probably wouldn't go looking for it elsewhere. My mother had warned me about that: "If you don't have sex with your own husband, he might go somewhere else to get it. Men need sex."

Our lives became normal. We talked, we played, and we were the picture-perfect young couple. Behind the picture, I was always perturbed at how scared I was to disappoint Prakash in any way after the night of the party. Our life was going well and I didn't want to do or say anything to tip it off balance.

The honeymoon, as I had anticipated, lasted only a month. Things changed all of a sudden. They changed the day Colonel Chaudhary was posted to Bhopal and came to our house for dinner.

Colonel Chaudhary had been Prakash's commanding

officer in Udhampur and Mrs. Bela Chaudhary was a perky, attractive woman who I liked at first sight.

After Colonel Chaudhary's arrival, everything changed. Not just at home, but also amongst the wives. They were gossiping as usual, only I kept getting the feeling that they were gossiping about me.

THIRTEEN

ANJALI

"I am sorry that Sarita brought . . . Prakash up," I apologized to Sandeep as we lay in bed. "I told her, and I—"

"That's okay," he said in his calm voice. He was lying on his back, reading a book. I was lying on my side, running a finger over his arm.

"You are angry about something." I could tell he was holding something back.

"Why should I be angry about anything?" He sounded amused, but I wasn't buying it.

"You've been angry ever since . . . we saw his wife."

Sandeep put his book aside and turned to face me. "I am not angry."

"Something is wrong."

"Nothing is wrong."

"I know you, something is wrong."

He sighed and lay on his back again. "You can really nag sometimes, you know?"

"I am learning from Komal."

Sandeep grinned. "She *is* pretty good at it."

"So, what's wrong?"

Sandeep closed his eyes and didn't answer. I poked him in the stomach with a finger. "Tell me."

He took my hand in his and brought it close to his lips. "I am happy. I am content. I am not angry."

"Promise?"

"Promise."

I turned off the lights and snuggled close to him. His body was tense and I lifted my head. "Something is wrong."

He laughed, this time uncontrollably, and I joined him. He never did answer my question.

Sandeep was not the most open person I knew. His feelings were locked within him, nothing gave him away, and I never knew how he was feeling unless he told me. He didn't express his emotions as freely as I did and it sometimes bothered me. It was a compromise—I got a close-mouthed clam, who was loving, affectionate, and understanding.

A few days before the *Dussehra* holidays I received a letter from my parents. I was shocked—the letter said they would come to Ooty for a week. It had been just a couple of weeks since I had written to them inviting them to our home. I had written several letters like this in the past. They had always politely declined my invitation with a reasonable if hastily contrived excuse. This time, however, I had written to them on Sandeep's insistence about Amar's failing condition, and the results were quite different.

Sandeep went to pick them up at the railway station and I crossed my fingers, praying that my parents' visit would go smoothly, without any unnecessary emotional upheavals.

I gave Amar a bath and dressed him up in a nice silk *kurta* pajama, which my parents had sent for him on his last birthday. Amar liked my parents and they adored him. Whenever we took Amar to Hyderabad, they treated him well, despite his illness. They took him on outings to the zoo, the planetarium, and the Birla temple that sat high up on a hilltop. Amar was inundated with gifts and trips to the ice cream parlors. I was thankful for their attitude toward Amar. He gave us a thread, a connection that was almost severed after my divorce.

I hadn't seen my parents for almost two years. The last time we were in Hyderabad we'd had a fight. I couldn't remember what the reason was—one reason mingled with another and one fight faded into the next. My parents never adjusted to my new life. They had found me a good-looking husband, an army officer with great prospects. I had blown that away and now had to settle down with a professor and a sick child. This was not the life they had planned for me. This was not the life I had wanted for myself. But I wouldn't change a thing—besides making my son healthy if I could. When they arrived with Sandeep I noticed that they had aged in the two years I hadn't seen them. They looked old and tired. As if they were ready to die.

My father seemed to have lost a lot of his domineering attitude. We'd never had a great relationship, but that was expected. Daughters didn't have great relationships with their fathers. He had thundered and raged when he found out I had filed for a divorce. He had wanted me to hang on to a bad marriage because their "noses would be cut off in society." I told him my life was too high a price to pay to save his idea of honor.

Now he seemed quieter, beaten.

Komal was a well-behaved woman with them. I probably appeared like a regular Jezebel, in contrast to Komal, who always wore white in deference to her widowhood. Komal was soft-spoken in front of them and very respectful, unlike me, and she followed all the religious rituals and had not left her husband or disgraced herself after his death by marrying again.

I was sifting the wheat flour for dinner when my mother finally tore herself from Amar, with whom she had spent most of the day in the living room playing, and came to talk to me. I knew she was going to talk to me instead of throw accusations on my face because she didn't start her words with "How could you . . . ?"

"He seems better," she said. "What do the doctors say?"

I ran my fingers through the soft flour. "His lungs are not getting any better and the heart operation . . . well, the valve is malfunctioning again."

"So . . . ?"

"We'll see."

She couldn't ask the question I couldn't answer. I couldn't even think it. He was sick and in pain, yet I wanted him to live just another day because in another day maybe science would catch up with his disease and cure him.

"Sandeep takes very good care of him," Mummy said. This was probably the first time she was saying something nice about Sandeep.

"He is wonderful with him and me. He . . . is so solid, I can really lean on him."

My mother nodded nervously. "He looks the kind. I . . . we came here because . . ."

"Because?" I prodded when the silence stretched.

Mummy smiled sadly, her wrinkled skin twirled around her face. "Daddy had a heart attack three months ago."

The sieve I was holding dropped and the flour rose like a small white cloud. How many people were going to get sick around me? I thought desperately.

I wheezed suddenly and it began. I tried to breathe but couldn't, and my mother's eyes widened in shock. Even before she finished calling Sandeep's name, he was in the kitchen with my inhaler.

Komal cooked that night while I lay in bed resting. Mummy sat beside me and told me what had happened to Daddy. It was his first attack and he would do better if he just watched what he ate, she said.

"Mummy, this is really bad news," I said.

"I know." She patted my hand. "And you've been through enough bad news, haven't you? I keep thinking how it must have been for you in Bhopal, lying in that hospital before we got there." Her voice was filled with sorrow. "I want you to know this because I know I haven't told you how I really feel. I believed you when you said Prakash . . . when you told us about him. I believed you. Your daddy still doesn't, but I believed you."

"Why didn't you help me then?"

My mother used the edge of her cotton sari to wipe her tears. "You were talking about divorce."

"And?"

"And?"

"Yes," I said. "He treated me very badly and he married me to avoid scandal and he was sleeping with another woman. A married woman. What did you want me to do? Be his wife despite all that?"

"Yes," she said unflinchingly. "You were his wife and marriage is forever. It is a relationship that is meant to be for seven lives and you turned your back on it."

"You still think I should've stayed with him."

She shrugged. "I see you with Sandeep and I am happy for you. Even with all your problems, you look happy with him. One heart attack and you should see how we are falling apart. I am scared he'll die and he's scared he'll die and . . . we aren't taking care of each other like we're supposed to."

"You'll be fine, Daddy will be fine," I said, and took a deep breath, enjoying the feel of oxygen. Since the gas tragedy one of my biggest fears was losing my breath, losing the ability to breathe. And after asthma attacks, I savored the feeling of drinking in fresh air as if it were for the first time.

"No," she whimpered. "He will die and what will I do then? Your brother is married to that cunning bitch. She won't take care of me."

I don't know what possessed me to say it, but I did. "I will take care of you."

"I can't stay in a daughter's house. What will people say?" she said, as if I had suggested that she commit murder. It was the rule: a daughter's marital house was off limits to her parents. A daughter never truly belonged to her parents; she belonged to her in-laws and her husband.

I grinned. "I got a divorce and fell in love and got married again. You really think I care about what people will say? You can stay with whomever you want and you can stay with me. But . . . Daddy looks healthy and we won't have to talk about this for a long time."

My mother was scared and I realized that her fears and mine were miles apart. I had come a long way from being just her daughter to the woman I was. If I hadn't made the choices I'd made, I would be like her, afraid to lose the only anchor in my life. I was terrified of losing Sandeep in some freak accident, but I was not worried about my survival if he passed away. I was not looking for someone to take care of me if something happened to Sandeep. I could take care of myself. Unlike my mother I wouldn't be searching for a place to live, trying to figure out who would be the best candidate to live with. Mummy knew after Daddy died she couldn't stay with me because she was worried what people would think; her only alternative was living with my brother.

Mummy never liked my brother's wife. Sanjay and I were estranged and he hadn't spoken to me since my divorce. It was amazing how my family had abandoned me, while strangers had opened their arms to me. I had always thought that the relationships we make with strangers are the hardest and the relationships we have with family the easiest. For me the opposite had been true. The family I was born into was not really my family anymore, while the family I made for myself out of strangers was mine.

"Sanjay still is just the way he was," Mummy went on. "He comes home with that woman and—"

"You arranged their marriage, Mummy."

117

"I know." She scowled. "But she was different then. She put on an act so that we would say yes. Once she got married, her true colors came out. She won't even let me see my grand-children. Whenever we want to visit them in Mysore, she says that they are going out to visit her parents in Chennai."

The irony of that didn't escape me. I invited my parents all the time, and they never came. They were drawn to my brother's family even though he didn't want them. The son was the heir, the one who was supposed to take care of the old parents, while the daughter was someone else's property unloaded at the first available opportunity on a husband and in-laws.

"She is just terrible. But the children—" She smiled. "—the older one . . . just so naughty and the younger one . . ."

She went on, telling me about her other grandchildren. The healthy ones.

Sandeep was adamant about not letting me do any housework that day. He went into panic mode whenever I had an asthma attack. I had tried several medications to cure my disease. But my asthma was related to the methyl isocyanate gas from the Bhopal gas tragedy—it was just one of those diseases that had to be "managed" and couldn't be cured. I probably would have dwelled in self-pity, but for Amar. The gas tragedy had hit him much harder than it had hit me, though he hadn't even been a thought the night I breathed the poisonous air.

"Maybe we should try the fish medicine again," Sandeep suggested. "It has been a few years since the first treatment, maybe . . . now it will work."

I cringed at the idea. The fish medicine was not pleasant. You stood in line for hours and someone dropped a live murrel fish stuffed with herbs and water inside your mouth, which you had to swallow. The treatment lasted three years, which meant once every year for three years I would have to go through the same ritual again. It was not a myth that people got cured. I knew several people who had recovered from asthma and bronchitis after the three-year treatment. It just hadn't worked for me.

"I don't know, it is a three-year commitment and I don't want to commit to anything right now with Amar not feeling all that well."

Sandeep raised his eyebrows. "But you want to choke all the time?"

"I am not choking all the time," I protested. "I am fine all the time. I am just . . . vulnerable—"

"—all the time," Sandeep finished. "You scare the hell out of me. I can't believe this. You haven't had an attack for almost a year and now . . . all of a sudden."

I shifted on the bed and got close to him. "Mummy told me Daddy had a heart attack."

Sandeep nodded. "He mentioned it to me. Asked me to take good care of you."

"They came here. That was a big step for them."

Sandeep muttered something unintelligible and I grinned. He was in a bad mood. It didn't happen often, so it was a novelty of sorts.

"I am fine. I can breathe. Look." I took two deep breaths to prove my point.

Sandeep was about to say something in response when Amar called out to me. He sounded distressed and we both rushed to him without further thought about my asthma attack. Compared to my son's illness, mine was the common cold.

Amar's chest was hurting and we gave him his medication to ease his pain. By the time he fell asleep that night, both Sandeep and I had forgotten about my asthma attack.

The rest of my parents' visit was uneventful—until the day before last.

In the parade grounds nearby there was always a big celebration for *Dussehra*, something Amar looked forward to every year.

We walked to the parade grounds, and Sandeep pushed Amar's wheelchair, my father walking with them, talking to Amar about the Himalayas and how much taller they were compared to the hills surrounding Ooty. Mummy, Komal, and I were walking ahead of Sandeep and Amar.

"I never thought this would be your life," Mummy said, as she turned to glance at Amar.

"Neither did I," I agreed.

"I never thought . . ."

I raised my hand to stop her. "I am happy."

"No, you are not happy," she mourned. "If only my children were happy. I must've done something wrong in some previous life. Otherwise why would both my children be so unhappy?"

Komal snickered and we both looked at each other with identical expressions of weariness. Mothers, I presumed, were the same all over the world.

"My mother used to always say that. She said that until

she died," Komal whispered to me. "She said it to Sandeep, too."

We walked silently for a while and then Komal leaned over again. "And we were happy when she was alive. Now . . . things are different."

"Sandeep is happy," I said tightly.

Komal looked at Sandeep and Amar and frowned.

We found a nice spot to watch the effigy of Ravana burn with the flames from arrows shot by young men standing below. Torn from the pages of the great epic *Ramayana*, it was the age-old story of good versus evil. It was on the day of *Dussehra* that Lord Rama, an incarnation of Lord Vishnu, had killed the demon Ravana.

Amar clapped when the first arrow hit Ravana and started a small fire. A few more arrows struck the effigy tied to a wooden pole and the flames rose high. Cheers went through the crowds and Amar was jubilant.

The parade ground was noisy and crowded. People were bumping into each other and the noise was deafening, but I heard my mother's squeak distinctly.

Instantly I worried that something had happened to my father and I looked to him. But he seemed perfectly all right talking to Amar and pointing at the burning effigy.

"I saw him," she said wildly, looking at me with big eyes. "He is here."

I tried to decipher what she was saying by following her line of vision and saw a man holding the hand of a young girl, looking straight at us.

Sandeep gave me a questioning look and I shook my head

in an effort to tell him everything was fine. I pretended nothing was wrong and Sandeep went back to looking at Amar's happy face. While I tried to make out what my ex-husband's daughter—healthy daughter—looked like.

❧ FOURTEEN

ANJALI

I always wanted to have children.

I wanted to have a child as soon as I got married the first time. Prakash didn't, so I went on the pill. That always made me uneasy, his nonurgency next to my urgency to conceive.

Why didn't he want children? Children meant permanency, a rite of passage into adulthood. I would be someone's mother forever and a mother was always an adult.

After the abysmal first summer of my marriage, I waited impatiently for Harjot to come back from college for the *Dussehra* holidays. We had kept in touch with letters for the past months and I missed her. She was the only real friend I had in Bhopal, and since things with Prakash had reverted back to how they used to be I missed her even more. I needed a shoulder to cry on, to help me sort this mess that was my marriage. I couldn't discuss my problems with the other wives who would gossip about them. Mrs. Bela Chaudhary initially had seemed like someone who could be my friend, but she was Prakash's friend and I was just his wife. I understood that they were close—after all, Prakash had served under her husband. Before we were married, he used to go to their house for homemade dinners. She had fed my husband when I wasn't there and I couldn't hold that against her.

I often saw them together. It all seemed like a coincidence, for the first few weeks at least. They would be talking at the Saturday evening *Tambola* party, and I would see them together at the Open Air Theater *samosa* stand. Prakash would go to get *samosas* during the movie's interval, and he'd leave the *samosas* with me and disappear for the rest of the movie.

I later found out that gossip amongst the wives had reached fever pitch while I was still naïve enough not to put two and two together. I couldn't imagine Prakash having anything to do with another woman. Middle-class men didn't have extramarital affairs.

When I went to play cards with Mrs. Dhaliwal and some of the other wives one day, Bela Chaudhary was there. Bela was in her early thirties, but she didn't look her age; she looked like she was as young as I was. I liked her. I couldn't help it. She was the kind of woman I wanted to grow up to be—sophisticated, elegant, and above all a woman who held her head high.

The other wives seemed nervous seeing us together in such close proximity. They probably didn't realize that I was stupid enough to like the woman my husband was having an affair with. Worse, they didn't realize that I didn't know he was having an extramarital affair.

She wasn't very good at rummy, while I had learnt the art of playing cards in the past few months. I helped her learn the finer points of the game. I taught her how to read, from the cards thrown down by other players, what sets the other players were making and how it would affect her game. I taught her what I knew and hoped that this would be the beginning of a new friendship.

As it usually was, the topic of discussion besides the card game at hand was movies.

"Did you see the new Amitabh Bachchan movie?" Mrs. Mehrotra asked, and silence fell.

"*Silsila,*" I said with a deep sigh. "It was wonderful."

Everyone shuffled their cards around, sipped their soft drinks, and tittered uncomfortably.

"What?" I asked, perturbed.

"Nothing, dear," Mrs. Dhaliwal said, as she dropped a card on the table. "It was a nice movie."

"I mean seeing adultery in a Hindi film," I continued. "I don't know how they could make the movie. It took a lot of courage to discuss that subject."

"I agree," Bela said.

It was a controversial movie. At that time it was rumored that Amitabh Bachchan was having an affair with the reigning actress, Rekha. In the movie he was married to his real-life wife, Jaya Bhaduri, and having an affair with Rekha's character. No one had dared to make a movie about adultery quite so blatantly before. The Hindi cinema still portrayed women as husband-worshipping wives and puritans. But in *Silsila,* the people were real, the circumstances were real, and the fact that the actors in the movie were facing a similar problem in real life added to its intensity.

I was playing the real-life wife in my small world, while

Bela was playing Rekha. She knew that; all the women sitting around the card table knew that; I didn't. So I talked about the movie and complained about the fact that the hero stayed with his wife when he was really in love with the other woman.

"So you think a man shouldn't stick to his marriage if he is in love with another woman?" Mrs. Sen asked.

"Absolutely," I said with conviction. "Marriage is sacred, of course, but if he is cheating on his wife, I think it would be better if he left her and married the woman he is really in love with."

I didn't know then that I actually meant what I said. I wasn't just stringing words together for effect; I truly believed in the sanctity of marriage and I did not want a husband who cheated on me.

Harjot came back to Bhopal for the holidays and didn't leave for a long time.

It was a mild October afternoon and, since it was the last day of the month, the kids had a half-day at school. Harjot was at my house telling me about the latest news from her college.

"But things are getting so difficult for us," she complained. Harjot was a Sikh and after Prime Minister Indira Gandhi ordered army troops to attack the Golden Temple in July, the Hindu-Sikh rift had expanded.

"But here, we are all the same," I consoled her.

In the army all religions were accepted. All holy days from Christmas to *Diwali* to *Id* to *Guru Nanak Jayanti* were celebrated. From what I had seen, no one noticed if you were Hindu or Muslim or Sikh or Christian. I had been shocked at how open-minded everyone was. In Hyderabad it was different. Not only did it matter what religion you belonged to, your caste was just as important. Being a Brahmin was better than being a Reddy and people from the same caste stuck together. I didn't have too many friends who were from the backward class. We mingled with our own people, but in the army I didn't even know what caste anyone belonged to.

Harjot and I were listening to Hindi songs on the radio, humming along with the singers and pointing out some of the bizarre lyrics, when we heard the bad news. One of our favorite songs from an old black-and-white movie was playing when a harsh voice cut off the song with a special announcement. Harjot and I groaned at the interruption.

When the harsh voice continued with the special news bulletin, Harjot and I knew she wasn't going back to college for a while.

We switched on the television immediately. There was only one channel and we devoured the news, staring at the television screen, afraid that if we looked away we would miss something. The downcast news anchor gave the nation the devastating news. Prime Minister Indira Gandhi was dead.

She had been assassinated by her Sikh guards. The guards she had been asked to fire by her colleagues in the Congress-I party just a few days prior. She had refused to fire the guards and had also refused to wear a bulletproof vest. She had said she trusted her guards and wouldn't insult their loyalty.

Harjot put her hand against her mouth in shock.

Tears pricked my eyes. This woman had been a constant in our lives and now she was gone. The great woman was no more. I kept waiting to hear more, for the news anchor to come back and tell us that it had all been a mistake and that Indira Gandhi was alive. I couldn't imagine the Independence Day parade without her, I couldn't imagine watching the news without her. She was a politician, no one I knew personally, yet she belonged to me as she did to everyone else I knew who was a Congress-I supporter.

"I am so happy," Harjot said, tears streaming down her face.

Shell-shocked, I looked at Harjot. Her words exploded in my mourning heart. How could she be happy?

"What?" I barely managed to say.

"I really am, Anjali. She made Punjab a battlefield."

"How can you say that?" I cried out. "She is . . . dead."

"And that makes all her mistakes right?"

I couldn't believe Harjot could think that Indira Gandhi's death was a good thing. "She was killed by Sikhs. Is that why you are happy?"

Harjot was the only friend I had had for months and I was arguing with her over a dead person neither of us knew much about. "Yes, actually it is."

"Really?" I asked, ignoring the fact that besides her I had no friends in Bhopal. "How can you be so unpatriotic? She was our leader."

"She was your leader, not ours. To the Sikhs she was just another Hindu tyrant," Harjot said, before she stormed out of the house leaving the door wide open. I slammed the front door shut.

The little bitch! I decided never to speak with Harjot again. She was a Sikh; what did she know about loving India? All Sikhs wanted their own country, wanting to break away from India anyway—traitors, all of them.

When Prakash came home, I burst into tears, partly out of anger and partly out of grief. I told him what Harjot had said.

"Colonel Dhaliwal has been saying things like that for a long time," Prakash said, and wiped my tears with his fingers in an effort to soothe me. "They are probably throwing a party."

"But he is an army officer," I protested, moving away from Prakash as anger took over again. I wiped away the remaining tears on my face and said sarcastically, "And I thought everyone in the army was green."

Prakash made a sound in disgust. "One would think so. But these Sardars are just . . . they killed Indira Gandhi. Heads are going to roll because of this."

Prakash was right. The riots began almost instantly. It was a massacre. The Hindus were outraged at the killing of Indira Gandhi and started slaughtering Sikhs wherever they could find them. News of Hindu mobs burning down Sikh homes with the people in them became rampant. News about Hindu mobs running around with swords beheading Sikhs became an everyday affair. The riots were worse in big cities, like Delhi and Bombay, with some of the anger and rage spilling into nearby states like Haryana, Punjab, and Uttar Pradesh. Bhopal, nestled in the center in Madhya Pradesh, didn't see much of the bloodshed because the population of Bhopal was largely Hindus and Muslims. But the cloud of despair and uneasiness encompassed the entire country and I mourned along with everyone else the needless death of Indira Gandhi as well as the brutal deaths of the Sikhs. I couldn't blame an entire religion because of what a few of their members had done.

However, my broad-mindedness did not include speaking with Harjot. I heard from Mrs. Sen that no one was speaking with Mrs. Dhaliwal either. Apparently Colonel Dhaliwal had thrown a party for other Sikh officers the day after the assassination. I was disgusted.

I vowed never to speak with Harjot again.

But I couldn't keep that promise to myself. And I was thankful that I couldn't.

Three weeks after Indira Gandhi died, the riots and the bloodshed hit very close to home. Bad news always travels fast and when I heard from Prakash what had happened, I had to see Harjot and be there for her.

Colonel Dhaliwal's relatives were trying to get away from Delhi. They wanted to come to Bhopal, where they could be safe from the riots. They managed to come halfway, but didn't succeed in reaching Bhopal—at least, not all of them.

Colonel Dhaliwal's four brothers, their wives and their five children, had been traveling together by train. All of a sudden, the train had been stopped. All the Sikh men were ordered out and butchered to death by Hindus right in front of the eyes of their wives and children. It was rumored that the Hindus were also raping Sikh women, and everyone in the EME Center agreed the same fate had befallen Colonel Dhaliwal's female relatives.

The door to Harjot's house was open. Everywhere I looked inside the three-bedroom army flat, women were dressed in white for mourning. A young woman held on to a young boy, her body wracked with sobs. The boy stood perplexed in his mother's embrace, looking around the room with astonished eyes. He didn't seem to understand why his mother was crying or where his father had gone.

Harjot was in a white *salwar kameez*, sitting on a straw mat in the living room surrounded by women in white. Her eyes were red as if she had been crying for a very long time. She didn't say anything when she saw me, she just walked toward me and hugged me tight.

I stayed with her for the rest of the day. I helped in any way I could. I cooked and cleaned and made sure everyone ate. There were several people in the house. The newly widowed wives, the five young children, and Harjot's parents and brother—all seemed incapable of carrying out the everyday tasks. The extent of their sorrow was beyond measure and there were no sympathizers except for a few other Sikh families. I was the only Hindu in the EME Center who had bothered to visit them after finding out what had happened.

When I got home in the evening Prakash was already there. When I told him where I was he got angry.

"They celebrated when she died. They deserve this," he thundered.

"No one deserves this, Prakash. How can you say that?" I said. "I may have to spend the night there, just to help out."

"You are not stepping out of this house," he ordered.

And for the first time in my dismal, half-assed marriage I didn't obey him. Harjot was my friend and I was not going to let Prakash's prejudices come in the way as mine had.

"Yes, I am," I said softly. "And the door had better be open when I get back."

"How dare you?"

"How dare *you*?" I turned on him. "All her uncles were

murdered, and instead of showing sympathy, you want me to turn away. What kind of a person are you?"

"I love my country."

"You just don't like the people who live in it. You can't just like the Hindus and not like the Sikhs. They are all Indians," I yelled. "And don't ever tell me what I can or cannot do. I don't stop you from doing anything, so you can show me the same courtesy."

I was shaking uncontrollably when I walked out the door. I didn't even know I had it in me. Prakash seemed to be just as shocked at my behavior as I was. He continued to try and stop me from seeing Harjot but I was stubborn and ignored him and everything he had to say.

The resentment I had been feeling for him since we married amplified with his behavior regarding Harjot's family. We fought about it for a few times in the first couple of days, but after that he muttered under his breath and I muttered under mine. For the first time in our marriage I was doing something he had explicitly asked me not to do and he felt impotent at making me bend to his will.

Instead of living like strangers under the same roof as we had been, the incident made us even more distant from each other as my slowly building apathy for him was replaced with immense dislike.

Harjot and I became closer as friends in the next week. Army officers and their wives came to Harjot's house and shook their heads in sympathy and left immediately. No one wanted to have anything to do with the Sikh officer who had celebrated Indira Gandhi's death.

"If people high up find out, Anju, there might be trouble," one army officer's wife warned me on her way out of Harjot's house. "This could damage Prakash's chances of being promoted. They will post him in some hell hole next time because of your behavior."

"I am helping a friend out," I said, and she shrugged.

"They are Sikh; right now they are the enemy."

Mrs. Dhaliwal couldn't believe that her friends, women she had played cards with and invited to dinner and lunch, were turning their backs on her. The line had been drawn. The army was green all right—just Sikh green and Hindu green.

"Thank you so much, Anjali," Mrs. Dhaliwal said when I brought her a cup of tea. She was sitting in the master bedroom with her sister-in-law who hadn't spoken since the incident.

"She just won't talk," Mrs. Dhaliwal said, wiping her tears. "I can't make her talk. I don't know how to."

I wouldn't know how to either. This woman had seen her husband being butchered and burnt alive, while she had hugged her daughter close to her, hoping against hope to protect her against the Hindus that were bent upon revenge. This woman who had probably been raped while her daughter watched could not be blamed for not speaking. What could she say?

Bela Chaudhary came around the same time to pay her condolences. "I am so sorry for your loss," she said demurely to Mrs. Dhaliwal. And then she left. They were all putting on a show of sympathy while most felt the way Prakash did: the Sikh officer threw a party when Indira Gandhi died; therefore his relatives deserved to die.

The whole country was in the same frame of mind,

blaming the Sikhs for killing Indira Gandhi and instigating the riots. It was as if Indira Gandhi's ashes had become a dark cloud and settled on the country.

"I don't like that woman," Mrs. Dhaliwal said as soon as Bela left.

"She's nice," I protested. "She is so beautiful."

Mrs. Dhaliwal frowned. "I am going to tell you something I shouldn't. But you need to know. Do you know why Prakash was posted out of Udhampur?"

"His tenure was up."

"He had been there just one year," Mrs. Dhaliwal said. Tenure usually lasted two years, but this was the army. Plans were altered unexpectedly. Prakash had told me so.

Mrs. Dhaliwal, however, told me the truth. "He was having an affair with Bela Chaudhary. That's why they sent him here. I am surprised Colonel Chaudhary was posted here. It was a . . ." She paused to assess the damage done to me by the revelation that my husband had had an affair with Bela Chaudhary.

I was staring at her, trying to make sense of her words. The world was moving around me in slow motion as I repeated in my mind what she had just said.

Affair? My Prakash? Nonsense!

"Well, everything was hush-hush and no one said anything," she said, and added, "and he seems to have reformed since he married you. . . . But I have heard some rumors that he and Bela spend time together."

I could feel each nerve ending in my body, each singing a different mourning tune. Images flashed through my head.

Prakash and Bela talking.

Prakash and Bela drawing away from each other when I had seen them together behind the officer's mess at a *Tambola* party—what had they been doing?

Prakash and Bela meeting by the *samosa* stand in the Open Air Theater.

Prakash disappearing for the other half of the movie.

Prakash and Bela . . . together!

"The commanding officer of the unit, Brigadier Joshi, asked Prakash to get married so that things would . . ." She patted my hand, understanding the searing pain that enveloped me. "You need to know, so that you can save your marriage. Fight for him and don't let that slut do this to you."

I nodded vaguely and left for home without even speaking to Harjot. When I got there, I had to admit the gods above wanted me to know something. It was an omen, a bad one, but an omen nevertheless.

Bela Chaudhary was standing with my husband outside my house. They were talking and Bela was laughing softly. It was a scene out of a B-grade Hindi movie. The wife was catching the husband with the other woman. Usually the wife forgave the husband and he came to his senses. Usually the husband realized his folly and came back to his wife because marriage was sacred.

"Hello," Bela said with a smile, and I almost choked with feeling. I actually liked this woman. She was screwing my husband behind my back and I liked her!

"Hello. Would you like to come in for tea?" I asked politely.

"Yes, please come in," Prakash said a little too eagerly.

I made the tea like an automaton, while they sat in the

drawing room. I added a plate of fresh *ladoos* to the tray and set it on the center table.

"You have been helping Mrs. Dhaliwal during this terrible time," Bela said, sipping her tea. I wasn't sure if she was accusing me of being a traitor to Hinduism, or if she was complimenting me for being such a Good Samaritan.

"Harjot is my friend."

"Yes, but you have to see the way things are. I mean . . . Colonel Dhaliwal threw a party. Can you believe it?"

Well, that cleared my doubts. She was accusing me and I didn't like her anymore. It had nothing to do with her feelings about Harjot. I didn't care what her stance on Indian politics was. I was furious with her for messing up my life. My new marriage! She was the reason Prakash had changed. Since she had arrived in Bhopal—how long had it been? two months, three?—Prakash had reverted to his old self.

"How do you know he threw a party?" I challenged.

"Everyone knows," Bela said brightly.

"How does everyone know?" I demanded. "It is like saying a married man is having an affair with a married woman—everyone knows, but no one specifically knows anything."

What I was saying had nothing to do with the party Colonel Dhaliwal had thrown. I knew I was being more blunt then any sensible married woman should be, but I wasn't in a rational mood. I wanted to vent my anger. I wanted them to know that I knew. The outraged wife would stop the mistress from stealing the husband away. She would not ignore the affair and wait for the husband to be reformed.

"Anju? What are you talking about?" Prakash muttered. He made a motion with his hand, asking me to shut up.

"The only way you can find out if a married man is having an affair with a married woman is if you are under the bed, where they commit adultery," I said, impervious to his eyes and actions. Nice Hindu housewives usually didn't talk about "bed" and "sex" this openly. "You would have to be at the party to really know that it happened."

Bela tittered self-consciously. "You should be a lawyer."

I almost said that she should be a whore, but I was raised to be polite to my guests—within reason.

After she left, Prakash charged at me. "What was all that about? She is a nice lady. Couldn't you be nice to her? Colonel Chaudhary used to be my CO."

I looked my husband in the eye. "I don't have to be nice to the woman you are having an affair with."

It was probably just a reaction to what I had said. I don't think he truly meant to do what he did, but whatever his reasons, it did not reduce the force of his slap. My body swayed a little with the impact, both physical and emotional.

We both looked at each other in bewilderment. He couldn't believe he had slapped me any more than I could.

I walked into our bedroom and pulled out a suitcase. I started piling my clothes in randomly.

"Anju, I am sorry."

I didn't respond.

"It was a mistake. Please . . . don't go. Please listen to me. Anju, I am so sorry."

I dropped the blue silk sari, which my mother had so lovingly given me after my wedding, and collapsed on the floor. I hid my face in my hands and sobbed.

Prakash sat next to me and awkwardly took me in his

arms. "I am so sorry," he whispered over and over. And I believed him. And that scared me.

I couldn't even leave him, I thought desperately. I loved my husband and I wanted to have a happy marriage, not a lackluster one like ours. I wanted babies and I wanted him to love me. And I wanted him to stop seeing Bela Chaudhary.

He promised he'd do all those things, and he even started talking about my getting off the pill so that we could try and have a baby.

For a week, things were perfect. And then they went back to normal.

It was then that I realized I could blame Bela, but she was not the real culprit. Her husband should be the one to accuse her. Prakash was my culprit and I his victim. I married Prakash with a pure heart and he had abused our marriage, our vows, and me. If it hadn't been Bela Chaudhary, it would have been someone else. Prakash couldn't help himself. What did wives of men like him do? I didn't know. But I could guess. Wives stayed home and made babies and ignored that their husbands were making love to other women.

Out of the blue, I asked Prakash to book me a train ticket to Hyderabad. I said I wanted to see my mother. He didn't discourage me. He bought my tickets and arranged for an army Jeep instead of a taxi to take me to the railway station. He even made sure I was settled inside my train compartment.

I asked him twice if he knew when I was coming back. "You'd better be here. The train gets in late and I don't want to be stranded at the station," I warned him.

He promised to be at the station when I got back. He said he couldn't wait for me to come back. He said he would miss me. But he hoped I would have a good visit and would enjoy seeing my parents again.

He even kissed me on the mouth before he left. I guessed he was going to cheat on me again.

P R A K A S H

If Mamta, my daughter, had not insisted, I wouldn't have gone to the parade grounds. But Mamta was just eight and didn't understand the word *no* very well. My son, Mohit, at the age of five, wasn't interested in *Dussehra* and burning effigies. He enjoyed playing with his Lego blocks, making trains and cars with them for Indu and me.

If Mamta hadn't been with me, I would have gone and said hello to Anju's parents. They were good people and had always been nice to me. But I would have said hello for another reason—I wanted to meet Anju's husband.

He was wearing a *kurta* over a pair of dark pants and epitomized the stereotypical professor. But he looked like a nice man—Indu was probably right, Anju did seem happy with her new husband.

There was another thing I was curious about. The boy in the wheelchair. Who was he? Not her son? A chill ran through me. If her son was in a wheelchair, she couldn't be *that* happy, could she? I found some perverse solace in that. The fact that even I realized it was perverted made my self-disgust rise.

Mamta told Indu all about the fireworks and the flaming arrows. Regardless of how many fights Indu and I had, with the children she was a perfect ten. I would've liked to have a mother like her. Doting, protective, encouraging, yet not overly so.

"She had a good time," I told Indu.

Indu was pleased. "I am glad you took her. Mohit's been complaining that you didn't take him."

I grinned.

"Daddy wants us to come to Delhi for the December holidays. You think you can get some time off, or should I take the kids and go by myself?" Indu asked.

I shrugged. "I don't know if I can go, I'll have to see."

"Why don't you ever come with us on vacation?" she demanded angrily.

I sighed. "Why is everything a battle with you? And you are being unfair. I do come on vacation with you. But I don't get the summer off—I am not a housewife."

"What is wrong with being a housewife?" she asked.

"You know, Indu, I am just not in the mood for this," I said, and Indu left me alone in the drawing room.

Why couldn't she be happy with me for once? Indu perpetually put me on the defensive. Anju hadn't done that—but she had changed after Colonel Dhaliwal's tragedy. When I looked back I was ashamed. How could I have been so insensitive to Anju and her needs? She had wanted to be with her friend, while I had been petty. That was when Anju had really started to leave me. I had been so angry a Sikh had murdered Indira Gandhi that I was taking it out on any Sikh who came my way without considering Harjot's or Anju's feelings. Then it had been popular for Hindus to hate Sikhs; now things were different. Now Hindus were supposed to hate Muslims. I didn't have much hate left in me. I was whipped.

I couldn't drag my mind away from the boy in the wheelchair. What was wrong with him? Was he sick? Or had he broken a leg?

I knew next to nothing about Anju's life. She had been my wife; we had stood by the god of fire during our wedding ceremony and promised to be together for the next seven lives. I was still possessive about her—I wanted to know everything about her. I felt I had the right.

Indu was right when she said I was the only divorcé she knew. I was the only divorcé I knew. There were probably one in a million of us and there were no guidelines as to how we should behave if we encountered an ex-spouse. I didn't know how to approach my ex-wife. For a while I didn't even know how to address her. Should I say "wife" when I talked about her in the past, when we were married, or should I always refer to her as "ex-wife"? If there had been other divorces around me I might have known. Someone would have come up with a system.

I didn't think of Anju as my ex-wife. I thought of her as Anju. What possessed me to go back to Bela Chaudhary, I don't know. But by sleeping with Bela, I ruined a marriage that could have been wonderful. But I did sleep with Bela— many times—after she moved to Bhopal.

This time no one warned me or told me what to do or

what not to do. And Bela was discreet. People wondered, but no one could say for sure that we were having an affair. Colonel Chaudhary treated me like a friend—but I am sure he knew. He had to.

Everyone had been silent about it, everyone except Anju. I'd expected her to be the most silent, to save face. But she clearly said how she felt about my relationship with Bela to our faces. I had thought she was a naïve young woman, who would put up with everything I dished out. And she did. But she didn't put up with the adultery, as so many women would have.

When she asked for a divorce, I thought she was joking. I thought that the gas had damaged her brain or something. But she was serious. Two weeks after the Bhopal gas tragedy I received a letter from her lawyer. I didn't even know she had a lawyer. The letter said that she wanted a divorce and the reason for divorce was stated as "incompatibility."

After reading the letter I charged into the hospital where she lay in bed with tubes sticking out of her body.

"What the hell do you think you are doing?" I demanded.

She breathed slowly, and I wanted to be calm and sensitive, but I couldn't.

"I want a divorce," she wheezed.

"I figured that out," I said sarcastically, and waved the letter I had received from her lawyer. "You are not getting it. I am going to make sure—"

She lifted a hand, the one with a tube coming out of it. "My lawyer said that I can get a divorce on the grounds of adultery. Would you like me to do that?"

I stared at her. "I don't understand."

"Yes, you do. You don't want me to name Bela Chaudhary in the divorce papers, do you?" Her voice was husky, as if every word took effort, yet she managed to dole out sarcasm.

"I haven't committed adultery," I flatly lied.

"You have," she said. "A divorce case will bring the matter to everyone's attention—they won't be able to ignore it like they have for so long."

She knew my career couldn't handle another scandal pertaining to the same woman. Mrs. Bela Chaudhary had been a misdemeanor the first time, the second time it would be considered a monumental crime.

I sat down next to Anju on the bed, planning to take another approach. "You are imagining things, Anju," I said, touching her fingers. "We are fine, you and I. Once you get better—"

"I want a divorce, Prakash. I don't want to be married to you anymore."

Her voice was so lifeless that it made me believe her.

"You are just not feeling well. Once you get better you will see things differently," I coaxed.

"I want a divorce, Prakash."

I dropped her hand and paced the floor by her bed. "We can't get a divorce. It is as simple as that. We will be fine. We've been married a very short time and things will work out. This time, I will make them work."

"You slapped me once," she said softly. "You cheated on me, you treated me with no respect. I want a divorce, Prakash."

Unaware of Anju's divorce plans, her parents arrived a day after I received the divorce letter. They had come to visit and take care of their sick daughter, but I changed their agenda. I knew they were going to be my strongest allies against Anju's divorce plans. I told them what she was doing and swore my innocence. They believed me. I knew they would—I was the son-in-law, I could do no wrong.

Anjali's parents tried to convince her and finally told her that if she got a divorce, she wouldn't be welcome in their house anymore.

She calmly told them that she already knew that.

I realized then that she had thought this through. This was not an impulsive decision. She knew the consequences and she still wanted out of the marriage.

She had told me that she didn't believe our marriage was real. "A real marriage," she said, "is based on love and respect. We are just legally bound—and that bond needs to be severed."

I visited her in the hospital every evening, trying to persuade her against the divorce. I hired a lawyer myself, who promised me that we could drag this into court and no judge would give us a divorce. We'd been married only a few months—we could still make it work.

Since Anju had been admitted to the hospital, Harjot had been a constant by her bedside. She left the room as soon as I walked in and came back as soon as I was leaving.

I caught her outside Anju's room once and thought if I could convince Harjot, she would convince Anju.

"Harjot, I want to thank you for—"

"I don't want to speak with you, Captain Mehra," she said before I could even finish.

"Why, what has she told you about me? I am not a demon, you know. I am a good husband and—"

"And that's why I saw you yesterday with Bela Chaudhary by the swimming pool. Your wife is lying half dead here and you are with another woman," she said with disgust. "Give her the divorce, or I will testify that I saw you kissing Bela Chaudhary. Then what will you do?"

"I never kissed her," I said, as my mind frantically tried to remember the places we had kissed and if someone could have seen us.

"How do you know what I saw?" Harjot asked. "Just give Anjali a divorce. Let her go."

"And what will she do? Roam the world alone?"

"The Hindu Marriage Act allows for alimony. You will help her, of course."

I laughed harshly. "If she wants a divorce, she can have it. But she doesn't get a *paisa* from me."

So I signed the papers and since the divorce was mutual, based upon incompatibility, everything worked out flawlessly. A flawed marriage that ended without any blemishes. The papers were bright white with clean black typewritten words on them, the lawyers were understanding and business-like, and even I didn't throw a tantrum. Anjali had threatened me and I had been threatened. She said she didn't want any alimony and I was childish enough to say that I wouldn't give it to her even if she needed it. Then it had been my revenge. Now it was my embarrassment.

I don't know how she survived after she left me. Maybe she sold her jewelry, but I wasn't sure. I knew that she hadn't gone back home to her parents. They had written to me, apologizing for their daughter's behavior. They said that they had tried to convince her but she hadn't listened. They didn't know where she was, but as far as they were concerned their daughter was dead. At the time I was glad to read that letter. She had gotten what she deserved, I thought.

Now I was old enough to see my mistakes and they were *all* my mistakes.

I looked out of the large French windows that lined our living room—it was dark outside. I glanced at my watch and sighed—it was late. Tomorrow morning, I decided, I would tell Anju's parents the truth. They probably still didn't believe her and blamed her for the divorce.

P R A K A S H

I placed a call to her husband's college and asked for Anjali's address. The man who answered the phone didn't know exactly where Professor Sandeep Sharma lived, but he knew the general area.

I hadn't been to that part of Ooty and I drove slowly, looking around, assessing the status of the neighborhood. When I got there, I asked directions from some children who were playing cricket on the asphalt road, with a worn-down bat and a tennis ball. They showed me the way to the professor's house. I parked the Maruti a couple of blocks away and decided to walk the rest of the way. Like a thief, I didn't want to draw attention to myself entering her house.

It was a nice house; a small wooden board with SANDEEP, ANJALI, & AMAR stenciled on it hung on the gate. I took a deep breath and opened the gate. It made a harsh rattling sound. I wished it hadn't made the sound because I needed a last-minute escape route. But the people who lived in the house had

probably heard the gate opening and closing. They knew someone had entered their garden and were waiting for the knock
on the door. The people in the house were probably peeping
through the keyhole or looking out of a window by now.

I don't have the courage to go through with this, I thought,
desperately wanting to run back to my car and drive away. Once
I was inside her house, I would have to tell them what I had
done and I didn't really want to do that. I would have to admit
that Anju had been right and I had been wrong—my male ego
was not prepared to make that admission.

It was a cool October day, yet I could feel a burn inside
my body. My ears were hot and my heart was thumping like I
had run all the way from my house to Anju's. Why was I here?
I knew why I was here. I wanted to know about the boy in the
wheelchair. I wanted to know all about Anju's new life as some
other man's wife.

I raised my hand and gently knocked on the door. Maybe
they wouldn't be at home; maybe they wouldn't hear the light
knock and I could go away, believing I had tried my best to tell
her parents the truth.

I was not that lucky.

I heard her voice. It was a soft lilting voice, like the voice
heroes sang about in Hindi films.

"Sandeep, can you get the door?" I heard her ask. There
was movement on the other side and my courage almost abandoned me. Not her husband, I thought frantically. Not him!
Anyone but him!

I then heard a young voice insist that he would open the
door. "I'll do it, I'll do it."

The door opened and I stared down into the eyes of a

boy. I took a step back—he was Anju's son all right. He had Anju's eyes.

"*Namaste,*" the boy said, holding his thin hands together. He looked weak, as if some grave illness had bested him. This was the boy in the wheelchair. Anju's son was obviously not a cripple, because he was standing in front of me. But I could see he was not well.

Indu was wrong, I realized; Anju was not happy. I would be devastated if either Mohit or Mamta looked this ill and needed a wheelchair.

"*Namaste,*" I responded hoarsely. "Could I . . ."

Anju's mother peeped through the doorway, and her face went white. "Prakash?" she gasped.

"*Namaste,* Mummyji." I shouldn't have called her that. It was appropriate to do so when I was married to Anju, now it was not.

"Come in," she said weakly, and the young boy stepped to the side.

A familiar head bobbed out of the kitchen and then went right back in. The head and the body came out a second later, with a plastic smile on the face.

"Hello, Prakash," Anju said carefully. "Amar, why don't you get Daddy from the backyard."

Amar smiled and walked very slowly, grasping the walls as he moved to get to the kitchen and then beyond. I didn't know what to say, or how to say what I thought I wanted to say.

"*Arrey,* Prakash?" My ex-father-in-law gasped as he walked into the living room from inside the house.

"What can I do for you?" Anju asked, talking over her father. Her mother sat down on the sofa, her face still pasty with shock. My ex-father-in-law sat down next to her, his expression mimicking hers.

The sofa was old, but well maintained. The rocking chair next to it looked inviting. The lamps on the tables next to the sofa were new, but the tables looked beaten and old. There was a dining table next to the drawing room in a cramped area. It had a plywood top, and the chairs seemed to have received new upholstery several times.

I looked at my surroundings in blunt appraisal. They didn't have money, but the house was cozy. Indu and I were well off, but our house was not cozy. It was a house decorated for parties and entertaining.

Anju knew how to make a house cozy. She had done it with our army flat in Bhopal. She had grown plants that died when she left. She had sewed beautiful curtains that I had torn in anger when she had lain in the hospital demanding a divorce. She had . . .

"Prakash, *beta*?" Anju's father asked again.

"*Namaste.*" I folded my hands together again and cursed the impulse that had brought me here.

"Prakash?" Anju inquired again, and I lifted my hands a little in frustration. I didn't know how to start. All my courage and resources had been spent on just getting here and now that I was here, I didn't know how to say what I knew I had to.

"I am sorry to disturb you, but I saw you yesterday at the parade grounds and . . ." I let my words trail away. I was a little scared about her husband showing up. But I wanted to meet him, compare myself to him.

"I wanted to talk you," I then said to Anju's parents.

"Please sit down. Would you like some tea?" Anju asked.

151

I didn't expect her to be so polite, but maybe she knew why I was there. But could she know? Was I that transparent? Had our short marriage given her an insight into me that I was unaware of?

"No thank you, I just had breakfast," I refused as politely as the offer was made.

Anju's parents seemed unsure of what to do. There was no traditional precedent regarding how to treat an ex-son-in-law. I could see their confusion and I was glad I wasn't the only one lost in this mire of ex-relations and protocol.

"Well, I will leave you alone," Anju said, and walked out of the drawing room into the kitchen.

I could see that I was not going to meet Anju's husband. The line was drawn. I was to talk to her parents and take my sorry face out of her house. She didn't want me here and I didn't blame her for that. But I had been her husband, damn her. I had some rights.

"I don't think we have anything to say to each other," Anju's father said. "Except that we are still very sorry for what our daughter put you through. But . . . you are probably settled now and so is Anjali."

Did the man have to apologize? By the time I finished what I knew I had to say, they'd be throwing stones at me.

"Please don't apologize," I said. "I came to tell you what really happened. It was not Anju's fault. I . . . was to blame."

Anju's father shook his head. "It doesn't matter what you did, she still should have stayed to make the marriage work. Once you had children, everything would have been fine."

"I didn't want children," I said lamely. "I wanted to wait a couple of years."

"And that was very wise," Anju's mother chirped, like a nervous bird set in front of a hungry cat.

Even after all these years, they felt it was necessary to please me. I was not their son-in-law anymore, but they were still being nice to me. I didn't even want to think what they had done to Anju after the divorce. But I knew what they had done; they had abandoned her and I had refused to give her a *paisa*.

"No," I said, taking a deep breath. "You see, I was in love with a married woman, Mrs. Bela Chaudhary, and . . ." I stopped because they both looked like they were going to have seizures. I licked my dry lips and continued. If they were going to have a seizure, they could have it after I said my piece.

"I was transferred out of Udhampur because I was seeing a married woman, and the brigadier there suggested that getting married would subside the scandal about my affair with Mrs. Chaudhary. So I got married. I didn't make Anju happy because I was in love with another woman," I said, looking at my shoes. They were not polished well, I kept thinking, as the words poured out of me. It was a nice diversion, because I couldn't bear to hear what I was saying.

"I treated her very badly and then Bela's husband was posted to Bhopal. I started seeing her again. Anju . . . Anjali . . . questioned me and I . . . hit her. Then she wanted to visit you in Hyderabad. I let her go because I wanted to spend more time with Bela. The night I was supposed to pick her up at the train station I simply forgot, and Anju almost died. I didn't do it on purpose, I didn't know that it would turn out to be the night of the Bhopal gas tragedy.

"I lied to you then and I am sorry about that."

I didn't look up after I was done, but I could hear them breathe and think.

"If she had been a good wife, you would have started to love her and you wouldn't have seen this other woman," Anju's father said. "I am sure she did something that—"

"Didn't you hear me?" I was shocked. Didn't the old man get it? "I cheated on her and I hit her. I left her to die."

"Men slap their wives around a little when they get angry," Anju's mother said. "That doesn't mean they are bad, that's how they show their anger. And about this other woman . . . things happen. But you make the marriage work, one way or the other. Every marriage has problems, but wives don't just run and get a divorce."

Her parents were insane. Completely out of their minds to still think that Anju was to blame. I realized that even if I had told them the truth earlier, they would have blamed Anju. It was the curse of the society. The woman was to blame. Always! If she was raped, it was her fault. If she was beaten, it was her fault. If her husband cheated on her, it was her fault.

I stood up slowly to leave. I wanted very much to grab Anju's father's shirt and make him understand what I was saying, but I knew it was futile. "Anju was not to blame. She was brave to have left me," I tried again.

"Well, it is nice that you have no ill feelings toward her," my ex-father-in-law said.

I moved to leave and then stopped. "Is that boy her son?"

Their faces lit up. "Yes," Anju's mother said. "Amar just turned twelve. Such a sweet boy."

I swallowed before I spoke. "What is wrong with him?"

"He has a bad heart and . . . they operated but it didn't help. His lungs are also bad." Anju's mother had tears in her eyes and Anju's father's face had become bleaker than before. I could see the pain in their eyes. "He is very sick. He is such a smart boy—but he isn't very strong. Anjali and Sandeep take very good care of him."

"What happened?" I asked.

Anju, who had probably been listening in the kitchen, walked into the drawing room. "You did," she said succinctly.

"Come again?" He couldn't be my son, he was twelve and . . . I started to calculate in panic.

"The gas . . . remember? I breathed in that gas and then a few years later I had my son. The doctors didn't tell me that any child I had could be harmed because of the gas," she said, almost without feeling. But I could feel her anger beneath the calm veneer.

"You left me there to die, but I lived. All I have is chronic asthma, while my son has a whole gamut of diseases."

I was speechless. Did she blame me for her son? Was I to blame?

"Is he . . . going to be okay?" I asked.

"No . . . we hope," Anju's mother said. "But he doesn't have much time."

"Don't talk like that," Anju protested. "He is getting treatment and it will work. He will . . . the treatment is good."

The boy was going to die. My eyes filled with tears and my heart started to race. I had forgotten about her that night because I had spent the evening with Bela. I had been tired when I got home and went to sleep. It just slipped my mind that Anju was waiting for me at the railway station. It was not done out of malice. I hadn't left her there because I somehow knew that she would almost die that night. It was not intentional. But whatever my reasons, she had a son who was going to die. It was my fault and I couldn't deny that.

"Now if you are done speaking with my parents, please leave. We are getting ready to have lunch," Anju said in a controlled voice. It was the same voice that had told me she wanted a divorce.

I wanted to say something before I left, but what could I say? What could anyone say in a situation like this? Would a mere "I am so sorry" do the trick? How did one apologize for an error as great as mine?

I nodded my head toward her parents and without looking at her walked out of her front door with fear and guilt burdening my soul. I now knew about Amar and his sickness and I knew who was responsible. I didn't know how I would live knowing this. Now I couldn't ignore what had happened that night. I had left her there and for years I had consoled myself that she had lived, but I couldn't do that anymore. She had lived, but at what cost? Her child was sick and dying and it was my fault.

The night of the Bhopal gas tragedy I had slept while Anju had fought for her life, and now she was fighting for her son's.

It wasn't fair.

I had slept that night. Peacefully, breathing clean air.

SEVENTEEN

PRAKASH

I couldn't go home. I couldn't go to work. I didn't know where to go. I didn't know how to face my children. They were around Amar's age and they were healthy because I hadn't left Indu in the railway station on the night of the Bhopal gas tragedy.

I had gone to Anju's house to find out about Amar and compare her husband to me. Compare? I was almost a murderer—there was no comparison.

I drove aimlessly around Ooty, going through narrow roads in between valleys and curvaceous roads around hills. I saw through the waterfalls, ignored traffic lights, and stayed out until late in the night.

Finally, tired of the day and my own company, I drove home.

Indu was waiting for me in the drawing room, wearing a "party" sari and jewelry.

"Well, at least you are home now," she jibed. "I had to go

157

alone to Brigadier Pradhan's daughter's engagement party and answer questions about you."

I ignored her. I had other things on my mind. I had Anju on my mind.

But Indu was my wife. She needed to know the truth. It was a little late for revelations, but I was burning with the need to confess.

I walked to the wet bar in the corner of the drawing room and poured myself a peg of Scotch. I downed it in one swallow and then poured and downed another. Finally I faced her.

"Where have you been?" she asked, looking me in the eye.

"I went to Anju's house," I said, without flinching or looking away. The Scotch was single malt and good. "Her parents are in town. I saw them yesterday at the parade grounds. I went to tell them the truth."

Her eyes widened questioningly.

"They think Anju was to blame for our divorce."

"And wasn't she? You said that she simply couldn't get used to army life and that—"

"I lied," I said, and looked appreciatively at the bottle of Scotch.

Indu smiled as if she had finally found a buried secret— one she had been looking for for a long time. "She divorced you."

"Yes."

"Why?"

"Because I was a son of a bitch." I poured myself another drink.

"Get me a drink, too," Indu said, instead of all the other things I thought she would.

We took our drinks out onto the veranda. I knew Indu was waiting to hear the rest of the story, I just wasn't prepared for what she might say when she heard it all.

I told her in as much detail as I could what had happened and how I had ruined my first marriage. I told her everything, except about Amar. I didn't have the guts yet.

Indu listened patiently, without interrupting. When I was done I looked bleakly into the darkness.

"You were very young," she said. "And so was she."

"But she didn't make the mistakes, I did."

"She married you. That was a mistake."

I chuckled. "You married me, too."

"Because I wanted to marry you."

"Why? I was divorced, not the perfect catch," I demanded.

She set her drink down. "I don't know why. Maybe I was in love with you. My parents thought I was—according to them no decent woman ever marries a divorcé."

"Are you in love with me now?" It was an important question, though I didn't know what I would do with her answer. I didn't know if I was still in love with her. I cared about her, because she was my wife and because she was the mother of my children.

When Indu and I got married, I promised myself I would not stray and ruin this marriage as I had my previous one. I had not strayed, but I wasn't sure if I hadn't ruined my second marriage all the same.

"I don't know if I am still in love with you," Indu said, then sighed. "But does it matter so much? We have a life, and we have children. We are hardly living in a movie. Love isn't particularly important."

We both fell silent for a few minutes.

"Are you in love with me?" she asked.

"I don't know."

"Do you want a divorce?"

I was shocked that she would even think it. "No."

"Good, because I wouldn't just walk away like your Anju did. I would make your life hell," she said sincerely.

I didn't doubt her. "But I didn't divorce Anju. I am not that type of a man. I—"

"Oh, you divorced her all right," she interrupted. "Don't you see, Prakash, you made her life miserable and you forced her into divorcing you. You didn't want to be married to her, so you created a situation where your marriage couldn't survive. And it didn't."

She was wrong, I thought defensively. I never wanted a divorce. I was married and I didn't like it, but I knew for sure that I would have come to terms with it.

"You married her because you wanted to avoid a scandal and then you let her divorce you. Don't tell me the divorce didn't create a big scandal."

"I told everyone that she only wanted to leave me after the gas tragedy. I . . . made it sound like . . ."

"She was a little mad? A little confused because of all that gas? Or did you just tell them that she was an imperfect wife and you were leaving her?" she asked, arching a perfect eyebrow.

I looked at Indu then. I had avoided looking at her while I told her my sordid tale. I was afraid of what I might see.

Even when Indu was being sarcastic and insulting, she was beautiful. She had borne me two children and she was still beautiful. Her slim body, her soft skin, her face, everything about her was beautiful. Anju on the other hand bore the scars of her life. Her face and her eyes reflected her experiences. Her clothes were not sophisticated as they once were. She didn't wear any makeup. She used to be beautiful and now she was just another average-looking woman.

"But people must have guessed the real reason," Indu continued, her full lips twitching a little.

Indu wore makeup—always. Anju didn't—anymore. What had I done to my ex-wife?

"Did you meet her husband?" she asked.

I shook my head.

"Does she have any children?"

"A son."

"Did you meet him?"

"Yes."

"So? What was he like?"

I shrugged.

"Why did you tell me all this, Prakash?"

I shrugged again. I had no answer to that question.

Indu fidgeted with her whiskey glass and then suddenly threw it out onto the garden. The glass shattered against a cement pathway.

Her face contorted as she tried to hold back what looked like an onslaught of emotions. Her eyes seemed darker than usual, bright, and her lips were pursed together as if opening them would open floodgates she wanted closed.

"I can't believe I married a man like you," she said after a long pause, after she seemed to be in better control of her emotions. "You cheated on your wife! Have you cheated on me?" Her voice was not soft anymore.

"No."

"How am I supposed to believe that?" she demanded. "How can I believe anything now?"

She dragged her hands through her hair, ruining her perfect chignon.

"You slept with another woman. Was it in your bed . . . the bed you shared with Anju? How could you, Prakash?" she asked, tears filling her eyes.

She had been calm up until now, talking as if she didn't care one way or the other about my first marriage. But she did care. She loved me.

"I was young and stupid."

"No one is that young or that stupid!" she yelled. "You cheated on your wife," she repeated in disbelief.

We sat there silently for several minutes before she spoke again.

"I need a large drink," Indu said, and I went to get the bottle of Scotch and a fresh glass for her.

She filled the glass and swallowed the searing liquid. She winced, but I wasn't sure what was hurting her more, the sudden intake of whiskey, or the sudden knowledge that her husband was worse than she thought he was.

In the past, every time she said how well she knew me, I used to be tempted to tell her the truth about my first marriage and myself. Just to wipe away her smugness. Now I had and I felt no relief, no pleasure, and no pain. I was in a limbo of emotions. Feeling nothing but numbness. What Indu would say didn't matter right now. A boy was going to die because I had left his mother to die. I couldn't get over that.

In a deep corner, in a very small deep corner of my mind,

I was glad Anju divorced me. If we had stayed married, Amar could have been my child and I would have had to live with a sick boy. I would have had to live with a boy whose life I knew I ruined. I would have had to watch the life being taken away from my child, breath by breath. And know that I was to blame.

"Did you love her?" Indu asked. Her voice shook and tears freely rolled down her cheeks.

"Don't cry, Indu," I whispered. "Your makeup is getting ruined."

✣ EIGHTEEN

SANDEEP

I didn't want to discuss my wife's ex-husband any longer, but Anjali's parents wouldn't let it go.

"He is a nice man, Sandeep," Anjali's mother told me. "He has his flaws, no doubt, but a wife has to make the marriage work. It is her duty."

They were here for just one more day and I didn't want to tell them to their faces that they were wrong, that it was not Anjali's duty to keep a bad marriage alive. Anjali had done the only thing she could do and I for one had no complaints about that.

"Yes, it is a wife's duty," Komal interjected primly. She had found out about the divorce. Anjali's mother was not discreet and after Prakash left, she had cried and wept and Komal would have had to be dead to have not figured it out.

"I can't believe you married her after knowing all this," Komal said, looking at me in disgust. "I don't know how I am going to stay here any longer."

I had had enough. "Then you can leave, Komal," I said. "Anjali did the right thing by divorcing a man who abused her and their marriage," I told her parents. "You should be proud of her."

"Proud of a daughter who cut our noses off in society?" Anjali's father demanded. "She ruined us. Our reputation will never . . . she just ruined us."

"But she saved herself," I pointed out sharply.

Anjali's mother shook her head. "Look at your own sister. Her husband couldn't give her children, but she didn't run away. She stayed with him and tried to make it work."

Komal flushed. "It was not easy, but I knew my duties as a wife. A divorced woman!" She shook her head disparagingly. "Sandeep, you should have told me. I would never have let you marry her."

"I am going to Gopi's house," I said, and left to join Anjali. She had gone there earlier with Amar when Komal and her parents had dug up the old dirt.

When Amar told me that Prakash was in the house, I had been tempted to leave the garden work and go inside to meet him. How would we greet each other? Would we shake hands? The curiosity had been there, but there had been reluctance, too. Part of me didn't want to know this man who had been my wife's husband.

Anjali hadn't spoken to me about his visit, she just left with Amar. Amar didn't know about Anjali's first marriage. He knew that she was in Bhopal the night of the gas tragedy and that was why he was sick. Anjali and I had discussed the matter for months: should we or shouldn't we tell Amar why he was sick? Finally we knew we had to. He was ill and he needed to know why. We didn't tell him that Anjali had been married to another man and he was satisfied with our explanation: Anjali was visiting a friend, Harjot Dhaliwal.

Amar knew Harjot, since she visited us often with her husband and children. She had two adorable daughters who Anjali and I had come to treat as our own and she and her husband treated Amar like their own son. Harjot was special to me because of what she had done for Anjali after the Bhopal gas tragedy. I didn't know Anjali then, yet I wished I could've done something for her. The helplessness grated on me. I loved her today but when she needed me the most I hadn't even known her.

Anjali and Harjot were still as close as they had been over a decade ago. They met during difficult circumstances. First Harjot had lost her uncles in the Indira Gandhi assassination riots and then Anjali had almost lost her life in the gas tragedy. Maybe it was helping each other through the tragedies that made their bonds stronger. After Anjali's divorce, Harjot had helped Anjali make a life for herself. She had helped Anjali sell her jewelry, write the entrance exams, and get a new education, which she could use to support herself.

When Amar was born, Harjot had been there in the hospital room, holding Anjali's hand and mine. She had stayed with us, talked to the doctors, and helped us come to terms with the pointless question: "Why our son?"

I wondered what Harjot would do if she knew Prakash had managed to enter Anjali's life again.

Prakash was making me lose my balance and my serenity by throwing my wife into emotional chaos. Anjali seemed to be slipping away into a void. I felt like she was being torn be-

tween her hate for Prakash and her reluctance to admit that
what she was feeling might not be hate. Maybe she had forgiven him for his past sins and maybe in some odd Indian
woman way she still loved him because he had been the first
man in her life.

But I could hardly tell Anjali how I felt. I was trapped
within my own reflections. She saw me as an infallible man, as
someone who never lost his perspective, someone who could
stay calm and be stable through a threatening storm. And I
wanted to be the man she thought I was. But I was fallible
enough to wonder if my wife didn't love me as much as she
loved her first husband.

I couldn't reconcile my insecurities with what I knew was
true. I knew she loved me. I knew she would always be by my
side. I knew I made her happy. But I was still insecure and I
wondered if she loved me as much as it took to stay by my
side, and keep her genuinely happy.

Anjali was a good wife, a great friend and partner. She
was a strong woman. I didn't know many women who had the
courage to rip apart a marriage because the man was in the
wrong. She had, and I respected her for that. But I couldn't
help thinking that a part of her regretted the decision. It didn't
have to be because of who I was, it probably was because of
who Prakash was.

I came across as the confident husband, as a man who was
sure of where he stood with his wife, and I didn't want her to
know that I was not confident enough, that I didn't know for
sure where I stood. I had my doubts and my fears. I was afraid,
too, of a lot of things. I needed her by my side to be strong, to

face every day. I needed her with me to see things straight and help me deal with our son's sickness. I needed her to make me smile even though I knew that Amar could soon die.

I wouldn't know how to live without her. I smiled, I ate, I slept, I breathed because Anjali was there with me. Because I was sure that when I woke up, she would be sleeping beside me. Because I was sure that when I came home from work, she would be waiting for me in the kitchen with a cup of *chai*.

I loved her very much and I was afraid she didn't love me as much. I had never thought that I was the kind of man who measured love.

When I got to Sarita and Gopi's house, Amar was sleeping in the spare room, while Sarita, Gopi, and Anjali talked in the drawing room.

"It is chaos at home," I muttered.

"Maybe you should stay the night here," Sarita suggested.

"No, we'll have to go home," I said with a smile, trying to diffuse the tense situation. "They are still our guests and I wouldn't want to leave anyone alone with Komal for too long."

Everyone laughed a little, and then silence fell like an ominous thundercloud.

"I can't believe he did this," Anjali said, as if the shock of it was finally sinking in. "Now Komal will tell everyone. I might lose my job if they know that I am not only divorced but I am still talking to my ex-husband under banyan trees."

I took her hand in mine. "She won't tell anyone."

"She will tell Mala and Mala will tell everyone else."

That could happen. Mala was our neighbor and Komal's gossiping friend. But I would make sure it wouldn't happen. Komal depended on me to take care of her and she would have to find her own home if she caused any big problems for my wife.

"Trust me," I soothed, and she bit her lower lip.

"My parents don't believe me. They still think he is a saint."

"They believe you," I said. "They just don't believe that you should have gotten a divorce."

"And stayed with that two-timing son of a bitch?" Sarita cried out. "To hell with your parents. If they are going to be so stupid about this, let them be."

Anjali laughed despite her misery.

Gopi and Sarita were looking at us with sympathy and I disliked that. Anjali's parents were being unreasonable, but we were being even more unreasonable by letting them get to us.

"Your parents leave tomorrow?" Gopi asked.

"Thank god," Anjali said, and grinned. "I want to see them when I don't and, when I do, I can't wait for them to leave. And this time . . . how dare Prakash come inside my house?"

"You should've thrown him out," Sarita grumbled.

"How could I?" Anjali said. "I have never thrown anyone out of the house. If I knew how, I would have thrown Komal out by now."

We all laughed at her weak attempt at a joke and started talking about other things, though Prakash's visit stayed on everyone's mind.

Why had he come? Was it to make his peace or to create trouble for Anjali?

Whatever his motives, Prakash had told the truth. He had bared himself in front of her parents, even though they had chosen to continue blaming Anjali. How could any parents want their daughter to be married to an adulterer? How could they not want their daughter to be married to a better man?

I knew Anjali's parents couldn't fully accept me because they had not married their daughter to me, they had married their daughter to Prakash. I didn't think they blamed me for marrying Anjali, but they did blame her. It was because of her rash decision that she now had an ex-husband who they didn't know how to deal with.

It had been difficult for me as well, to deal with the concept of an ex-husband. But I had come to terms with it. It never bothered me that my wife was not a virgin when we married. It didn't seem important.

I couldn't reconcile the Anjali who was my wife with the Anjali who was Prakash's wife. They seemed like two different people.

She had lost her innocence and that angered me, not because I didn't get an innocent wife, but because something so bad had happened that Anjali's innocence was replaced with cynicism. I wish she hadn't lost so much.

A N J A L I

I was furious with Prakash. He had come to tell the truth without caring about the consequences. He had given me enough trouble in my life. Did he have to add to it now?

My parents continued their nonsense until they left. How could they talk about my ex-husband while my present husband was around? I knew my parents didn't respect Sandeep. A respectable man didn't marry a divorcée. But I was happy with him. Happier than I had ever been before. How couldn't they see and appreciate my happiness?

Prakash had come to relieve his guilt and had expanded my problems. Komal followed my parents' behavior and continued to bring up my divorce. Since we couldn't have a conversation without Komal mentioning what a terrible Hindu woman I was, I stopped speaking with her.

Amar I am sure sensed something was amiss, but he didn't ask what it was. We had always been honest with him and he knew that if it was something he needed to know, we would tell him.

At school I kept waiting for someone to talk about the divorce. But so far it looked like Sandeep had managed to keep his word. Komal had kept the juicy gossip to herself and no one was asking me questions about my ex-husband.

I wondered why Sandeep had not come inside the house to meet Prakash. Amar had told him that someone named Prakash was in the house. Sandeep hadn't even looked up from his shoveling in the backyard. He had asked Amar to help him pick out weeds and they had had a wonderful, though tiring, afternoon, according to Amar.

It had been bad enough dealing with Prakash when my parents had come to Bhopal and I had been demanding a divorce. It was worse now, because my parents could see the "what if's." My mother complained that I was not a brigadier's wife. If only I had kept my head and made no rash decision, I would have been married to a brigadier.

"It would have been a matter of such pride," my father had said. "Your being a brigadier's wife would have given us so much prestige."

Pride? Prestige? Sometimes I was convinced my parents were naïve and other times I was convinced that they hated me so much they wished me the worst in life.

I saw Prakash's wife again in the market. Since the first time I had seen Prakash and his wife there, it had become a habit to look around. It was a perverse kind of longing to see her and there she was again. This time wearing a dark maroon *salwar kameez*, her face made up, and glittering gold hanging from her ears, neck, and wrists. She was buying tomatoes and examining them in her perfectly manicured fingers.

Was she living my life? I wondered.

If I hadn't been caught up at the railway station that night I am not sure I would've pushed for a divorce. But I had seen people die around me that night. I had seen the city of Bhopal turn into a cemetery for months to come after the incident. Mass burials had taken place and I couldn't shrug the thought that I could've been one of those bodies piled up against one another, buried anonymously, or burnt to a cinder without any last rites.

It hadn't taken long for me to realize how precious life was and that I didn't want to live the rest of mine with Prakash. It was the well-known cliché: a brush with death brought everything into perspective. After seeing what I had seen the night of the gas tragedy, I knew what I had to do and I knew that every breath I took was leading me to death, untimely or otherwise. Time was limited, and I couldn't count on Prakash changing while I wasted my life putting up with his abuse and adultery.

But his second marriage seemed to have survived. His wife didn't look like a young woman and the girl at the parade grounds with Prakash was around seven or eight years old. Indu had stayed married to him and I had run. Was everyone right? If I hadn't given up on our marriage, would things have finally worked out? Would I be wearing expensive clothes and jewelry, instead of an old cotton sari and no jewelry?

I stared at her through the crowd and suddenly, as if

pulled like the sea to the moon, her eyes met mine. There was a moment of recognition in her eyes and then we stood still. I wanted to walk up to her and ask her if she was happy with Prakash. I wished she was unhappy so that my decision of leaving him could be justified. I wished that their marriage was as bad as ours had been. I wished that he was callous, rude, and insensitive, and I wished that he cheated on her as he had on me so that I didn't have to wonder about my choices.

She walked up to me and I wanted to run, disappear into the people and the bazaar. But I stood, rooted to the ground.

"Namaste." She smiled and I nodded. "How are you doing?" she asked.

"Fine," I replied. The ex-wife and the wife were having a polite conversation—I had never heard of anything so ludicrous.

"How are you?" I asked.

"Fine."

We stood there like comrades who had been enemies in some previous battle. Now the wars were over and we could shake hands across the border without hating each other or the thought of each other. She had hated me—she must have, because I had hated the idea of her. Now we didn't have to hate because the curiosity had been satisfied. I knew her and she knew me, we had seen each other. We were not afraid.

"Did your parents have a nice visit?" she asked, and my eyebrows went up. He had told her?

"Yes, it was nice." Until your husband came by, I thought silently.

"I hope Prakash . . . didn't cause any trouble," she said, and I had to admit that she was a whole lot more perceptive than her husband. On the other hand, she was a woman and

she understood the niceties of society better than an army officer who had gotten his way most of his life.

"Some . . . he caused some trouble," I said emotionlessly.

She looked down at her feet and then raised her face. "He
is very sorry for what he did. All of it."

I looked around trying to breathe because it was getting
very suffocating.

"Why are you talking to me?" I finally asked.

"Because I am sorry that he did what he did and . . . I
don't really know why I am talking to you," she admitted with
a faint smile. "This is very awkward."

"Yes," I said.

We stood in silence for another minute or so.

"It was . . . nice meeting you," she said.

I nodded and watched her go back to the vegetable stall
where she had been standing.

And just like that, a weight was lifted from my shoulders.
No, I didn't want her life. I hadn't wanted her life even when I
had had it. I didn't want to be with a man I needed to apologize for.

Her apology had cleared me of any blame. I stood in the
middle of the market, smiling like a fool.

Komal refused to eat dinner. She had thrown some tantrum
about the cauliflower curry not being to her liking and had ex-
cused herself from the table.

Amar could barely sit up these days, but he insisted on
eating with us. He had trouble breathing all day and his medication was not helping. It happened once in a while and threw

us into a state of panic. Sometimes his breathlessness escalated and he needed to be hospitalized. The last time this had happened was two months ago. I had been keeping count and the frequency of how many times we had been to the hospital in the past year because he couldn't breathe had increased. Earlier it used to be once in six or seven months, but for the past year it had become more regular. Almost every two months and sometimes every month, Amar needed to be hospitalized for a day or two, sometimes longer.

I was folding the laundry before going to bed and Sandeep was as usual reading the newspaper, when I broached the subject we didn't want to ruminate over. Amar was getting worse every day; neither of us wanted to face that.

"I hope he doesn't have to be taken to the hospital," I said with equal amounts of fear and concern.

Sandeep put the newspaper aside and patted the bed. "I'll fold them tomorrow, come here."

I left the laundry and crawled into bed to sit beside him, my legs crossed.

"It is temporary, he'll be fine soon. He always gets better." Sandeep didn't believe it himself and I could see it in his face, his eyes.

Amar had been failing with every passing day. He had been failing ever since he was born. Every day I kept my fingers crossed as I heard with sinking hope the small wheezing sounds he made as he breathed. And a question inundated my every conscious and subconscious thought: would there be time for a miracle for my son?

"I met his wife today," I said, not looking at Sandeep. "She actually came to speak with me."

"What did she say?" There was no surprise in his voice.

"Hello and that . . . he is sorry for everything."

"So she knows," he said.

"I think so."

I then raised my eyes to meet his. "I am glad that I divorced him."

"You say that like you just got glad about it and weren't earlier?"

"I was glad about it; I am still glad about it. It is just sometimes when my parents keep hounding me, I wonder . . . that's all," I said, trying to explain what I had realized in the bazaar.

"What do you wonder?" Sandeep asked, his voice dropped to a whisper.

"That maybe I was hasty, that the gas tragedy made me look at things . . . in a . . . skewed light," I said, struggling with the words.

His eyes widened. "Have you been unhappy all these years with me?"

"No!" I exclaimed. "This is not about us. I have never been happier, more content. Even though Amar is sick, this is the happiest I have ever been."

He got out of bed and paced the floor. I had never seen him this agitated before. A part of me was thrilled that I had managed to finally break him down to the extent he was losing the calm veneer that covered him from head to toe. Another part of me felt guilty for making him feel this way.

"I haven't given you a good life," he finally said, revealing his insecurities. Insecurities I never associated with him.

"What makes you think that?" I asked, shocked.

177

"You have . . . very little." He shrugged.

"I have a whole lot more than I ever did," I countered. "How I feel about my choices has nothing to do with my marrying you. They were . . . frozen—part of that time when I divorced Prakash. My parents, Prakash, the officers' wives, everyone seemed to believe that I was a bad wife because I didn't want to be his wife anymore."

"You've been a great wife to me."

I smiled. "I hope so. I love you, Sandeep."

"But you loved him, too," he pointed out.

"I am not sure anymore what I loved, the army officer or the man beneath that olive green uniform," I confessed. "I was young and I thought that marrying Prakash was what I wanted. I regretted the marriage and I got out of it. I am glad I did. It was the right decision—it was a brave decision. I don't know where I found the courage.

"Today when his wife apologized to me, I knew that what I remembered was not a jaded, one-sided picture. He did hit me, he did cheat on me, and he did not hold up his end of the marriage bargain of being a good husband.

"Which is well and good for many women and it probably would have been for me, too. I'd be a brigadier's wife apologizing to the women Prakash mistreated. But I came too close to death and . . ." I didn't know what to say anymore.

I had said it all before and I didn't know if he could see the enlightenment that had been bestowed upon me. I was seeing the past like I had never been able to see it before. I always blamed Prakash for what had happened to our marriage and to me, but I had also blamed myself, wondering if the people around me were right. If only I had persevered and stayed, my marriage with Prakash would have worked.

"Do you know *now* that you made the right decision by divorcing him?" Sandeep's voice was forceful and demanding.

I shook my head. "I always knew it was the right thing, but . . . people don't make it easy for a divorcée, Sandeep. Komal thinks I am to blame and I have had to listen to that ever since I divorced Prakash, from many people. I had doubts and . . . damn it, they were justifiable."

"So when you married me you were not sure if divorcing Prakash was the right thing to do?"

Why was he was being so obtuse? Why couldn't I make him understand that now I didn't feel like I was to blame for the failure of my first marriage? What did that have to do with my marriage with Sandeep? I felt helpless, unable to make him see how I felt.

"No, I was not sure . . . not entirely," I snapped. "Happy? Is that what you wanted to hear?"

"No, what I wanted to hear was that you love me so much that it doesn't matter whether divorcing Prakash was the right thing or not," he said, his eyes bleak. "You have always been fascinated with him and ever since you saw him again . . . I feel like you have been wondering if maybe life with him would have been better than what you have with me."

"That is not true!"

"Why do you want me to hate him, Anjali?"

"Because I hate him. Because of what he did to me . . . to Amar."

He laughed without humor and shrugged. "I don't think

you hate him. I think you are obsessed with him. You want me to hate him in your place, because you can't."

"Is that how you really think I feel?" I demanded.

"You don't hate Prakash. You've never hated him. He is the man who shattered your dreams, but he is also the man who was there first," Sandeep said with passion. "And maybe somewhere in that soul of yours you feel that he was the right choice, I was the wrong one."

I was speechless for a few seconds.

"I can understand your regret at marrying me—" he continued, when I jumped out of bed and interrupted him.

"I never regret marrying you," I cried out. "I just wasn't sure if the divorce was . . . the right . . . the only thing to do."

"It is the same thing, Anjali."

He had never been this difficult before. We had lived a comfortable life with little thought of the past, until Prakash showed up in Ooty.

"It is not the same thing," I said weakly.

"Are you telling me you've never looked at his wife and thought that she is living your life?" Sandeep demanded.

"I don't want her life!" I yelled. "I had her life and I didn't like it one bit."

"And it took you over fifteen years to figure that out," he argued, yelling just as loudly as I was. "Our marriage was always shadowed by the doubts in your mind."

"Are you telling me that this has been on your mind all these years? I thought our marriage was perfect." I was furious.

"Oh, I never realized that it was shadowed by your divorce until now," he said. "But in your mind it always was."

"And what if it was, how does that matter?"

"It matters," he said. "Even if I didn't feel it until now, you did and that . . . that, Anjali, is the issue."

I couldn't believe he was saying all this. He seemed to be convinced that I regretted leaving Prakash, that I regretted marrying Sandeep.

"I love you, Sandeep," I said, calming myself down. "I have always loved you and I have only loved you. I had an arranged marriage in which love was not a priority. I divorced Prakash because our marriage was dead. The doubts in my mind were not mine, everyone else around me planted them. How strong do you want me to be?"

Sandeep ran a hand through his hair in frustration. "I thought I had a whole wife, Anjali. If you were divided, you should have told me."

"I didn't know myself until now," I said. "I didn't even think about Prakash until I saw him again."

Sandeep seemed to contemplate that for a minute or so and then, as if he had reached a decision, he looked into my eyes. "Would you go back to Prakash, now that he has proved he has some twisted version of integrity? After all, he did come and tell your parents the truth."

I stared at him in shock. "That was not integrity, that was guilt. And I am already married."

"What if you were not married?"

"That is an unfair question. But if you must know, no, I wouldn't go back to Prakash. I learn from my mistakes," I challenged him.

Sandeep pulled me into his arms and kissed me. He understood, he didn't have any more doubts, I thought happily.

Sandeep was always so certain of himself, of our marriage,

of me, that his doubts that seemed to have appeared out of nowhere made me appreciate him even more. He had doubts, too—he was not infallible, as I had always thought him to be. His emotions were as fragile as mine were and I realized that I had been treating him without any regard since Prakash had entered my life again. I had selfishly exposed him to my feelings, without considering his.

I clasped him tightly, wanting to protect him from his demons. He was human after all and I had expected him to be some god, who could bear it all.

"I love you," I whispered.

"I just needed to know." He sounded contrite.

"I needed you to know."

We made love in a frenzy, tearing at each other's clothes, urgently needing the closeness that we both were afraid we might have lost.

"I never really doubted you," he said, catching his breath.

"I know." I smiled.

It was early in the morning when Amar woke us up.

"Mummy, I feel funny," he said as soon as I entered his bedroom.

"Funny, ha, ha, or funny, peculiar?" It was a game we'd played for years and he usually laughed when I said that.

"Funny, peculiar," he said, clutching his chest.

I saw his pale face and cried out for Sandeep.

✺ TWENTY

PRAKASH

"Why did you talk to her?" I yelled in disbelief. I knew she was capable of doing something this brazen, I just thought she would have the better sense not to.

"I wanted to apologize on your behalf, Prakash," Indu snapped. "And don't yell at me, my head hurts."

"You've been drinking yourself silly for the past few days. What is wrong with you? Women don't drink!"

"Really?"

"How many women do you know who drink? And I am not talking about your card game circle," I said forcefully. Drinking alcohol was a new fashion amongst army officers' wives. In the good old days when I had first been commissioned, women who drank were frowned upon; now no one seemed to care.

"I don't care who drinks and who doesn't. How many women do you know who are married to divorced men?" Indu retorted.

"Are you going to bring that up for the rest of our lives?" I demanded, regretting the attack of conscience that had made me tell her the truth about my first marriage.

"No, just for the rest of your life," she said, picking up the copper ashtray lying next to her and throwing it at me. I didn't even have to duck to avoid it. Indu had terrible aim. Always did.

The ashtray fell on the mosaic floor of the living room and clamored before settling into inertia.

"You shouldn't have talked to her, Indu. It is none of your business," I said softly. "She is in the past and it is over. . . . Can we please move on?"

Indu smiled cynically. "Move on? It is so easy for you to say that. It is so convenient to just push it under the rug and . . ."

I raised my hand to silence her. "Enough, Indu."

"Did you even think what would happen if you went to her house to talk to her parents? Did you even stop to consider what problems might come her way?"

I hadn't, but I didn't want Indu to know that, so I shrugged with indifference.

"Ooty is a small place, Prakash, and she is a schoolteacher. If people in her school knew she was a divorcée, do you think it might cause some problems for her?" Indu asked.

"I did what I thought was right." But her words had hit the spot. As usual, I had been selfish, thinking about myself and no one else. I had been doing it for so long, it had become a character trait, almost as if it was genetic.

"You did what you thought was right," she said, her tone laced with sarcasm. "You infidel son of a bitch—"

"Are you fighting?" my daughter's tiny voice interrupted

Indu. She was peeking into the living room from the hallway. Her eyes wide, questioning, and her lips set mutinously.

I opened my arms and Mamta ran into them. I swung her up high and then held her. "No one is fighting, *beta*. Mama and I are just talking."

She moved her face away to look at me and raised an eyebrow comically. "What does in . . . fi . . . de—"

"Means nothing," Indu snapped, then smiled at Mamta, who appeared to be ready to take issue with the snapping. "Nanima sent some *ladoos*. Do you want one?"

My mother-in-law often sent sweets or clothes or something else for the children. Indu was an only daughter, and a spoiled daughter she was. When Indu and I announced that we were getting married, her parents had tried everything they could do to stop us. I even had to meet with her father, where he threatened me with dire consequences if I didn't leave his daughter alone. When I told Indu about the conversation, she raged at her parents for days and, finally, her doting parents gave in to their darling daughter's desire. They married her off to me and never again showed even an iota of disapproval.

Now after all these years of marriage, they had even started to like and appreciate me. Though they probably always thought that Indu could have done so much better than to marry a divorced man.

Mamta forgot about our loud voices and went inside the kitchen, squealing loudly about the sweets.

Had I done too much damage to Anju's reputation? I must have. Anju's parents refused to see me as the bad guy. They were still convinced it was her fault because she hadn't tried hard enough to make our marriage the roaring success they thought it could have been.

I decided to go to Anju's house the next day and talk to her and clear it up. I wanted to let her know that I hadn't wanted to cause any trouble, I just wanted to let her parents know the truth.

I slept in the guest room that night because Indu locked the door of our bedroom from the inside. For someone who had calmly married a divorced man, she was certainly behaving strangely. Was she angry because she now knew that it was Anju who had divorced me? Or was it the reason why Anju divorced me that bothered Indu?

I hadn't told her about Amar yet and now I didn't have the courage to do it at all. She would probably kick me out of the house if she knew I was the reason a young boy couldn't walk by himself and was going to die.

I had never been Indu's hero. She was the antithesis of Anju. She didn't hero-worship army officers; she had been raised in the army. I knew that with Indu there would be none of the shenanigans that Anju had tolerated and that was one of the reasons why I had married her. Indu was a stronger woman, not supple and naïve like Anju. Well, the Anju who had married me. Toward the end she had not been naïve and supple. I had hardened her and made her cynical and cold. Maybe her new husband was a better man—but I didn't really want that myself.

On a baser level, I wanted to be the only man in Anju's life because I had been the first. Since that was not possible, I hoped that her new husband was no better than I had been. I wished that her second marriage was no better than what she had had with me.

The next morning I left the house before Indu woke up. She had stayed in our room all night and I knew things weren't going to be any different for a while. I had never spent the entire night alone in the guest room, but this time I had. Usually when we fought Indu would join me and cajole me into a good mood. Usually Indu would be the one at fault and she would always apologize and then we'd make love. I knew that this time Indu thought I was at fault and I should be the one to apologize. But I hadn't done her any wrong. I had been the best husband and the best father I could. I had never cheated on Indu or abused her. I couldn't understand why she was so upset.

I hesitated when I told my Jeep driver where I wanted to go, but I ended up at Anju's doorstep once again. I had come from my office and was in uniform, my stars shining, my clothes neatly ironed—I looked like the brigadier I was. For a while I had even worn a moustache to complete the army officer look; but Indu said it tickled and I had let the moustache go.

An older woman, in white, opened the door.

"Can I speak with Anju . . . Anjali?" I asked politely, suddenly remembering she would be at school. I was so used to thinking of her as a housewife, I had forgotten she now worked. How modern! She used to hate the idea of working outside the house—she used to believe that the man should bring home the money and take care of the bills and provide for the wife and the children.

Was Anju working because she and her husband needed the money? Of course she was, I thought smugly. With a sick son at home, wouldn't she rather be at home, instead of working for a meager schoolteacher's salary?

The woman who opened the door looked at me suspiciously, and for a moment I thought that she would shut the door on my face.

"She is a married woman now," she said angrily, and I nodded.

"I know, I just wanted to talk to her or . . . her husband." I added the husband part to convince her that I was here on honorable business.

The woman sniffled a little, as if at the brink of tears.

"They are in the government hospital. Amar, my nephew, fell very sick early in the morning."

I felt my stomach fall down. "How sick?"

"We don't know. Sandeep said he would come home . . . and tell me." She started to cry. "That boy is pure gold. Nothing bad should happen to him."

"I will go . . . to the hospital and check," I said impulsively. And once I said it, I knew I had to do it. That boy was there because of me. He was my responsibility, too. "And I will make sure someone lets you know how he is doing."

I got back into the Jeep before she could say anything and instructed the driver to go to the government hospital and to make it fast.

The hospital, like all hospitals, smelled of disinfectant and medicines. The hospital, like all government hospitals, was dirty and messy. Sick people were lying on the floor because there weren't enough beds to accommodate the poor. It seemed infested with diseases. This place would make a healthy person sick. Why the hell would anyone bring their child here?

I knew the answer to that one: lack of money. I was used to military hospitals that were sterilized and everything was done with the precision the Indian army was known for. This was a far cry from the clean military hospital I had taken Mohit to a month ago when he had a fever.

It was easy to find Anju. She and her husband were in the lobby of the intensive care unit. I assumed that their son was in one of the ICU rooms.

Anju was sitting on a bench with her husband. He had his arm around her and they were rocking each other, comforting one another.

He saw me first. I was noticeable in my uniform and he moved his head in acknowledgment.

She raised her head slowly and her eyes fell on me. For an instant she was shocked and then she flew toward me in a rage.

"What are you doing here?" she yelled, ignoring a nurse who tried to shush her. "Go away! Get the hell out of here. Now."

I stood there helplessly. "I . . . went to your house . . ."

"Go away!"

The nurse looked at me angrily and motioned toward the door.

"He is going to die," Anju yelled. "Do you know that? Did anyone tell you that? Is that why you are here? To see?"

"No," I said hoarsely. Tears filled my eyes and clogged my throat. "I . . . I wanted to make sure he was okay."

"Why? What is he to you?" she demanded acidly.

Her husband came and stood beside her. He put his arm around her and she collapsed against his shoulder, whimpering softly.

"I just wanted to check," I said to her husband because she didn't seem rational. "I . . ."

"I think you should leave and maybe . . . come back later," her husband said politely and calmly. "She has had a—"

"Don't come back later. Never come back. This is because of you." Anju's head reared up again. "You left me that night and now he is going to die. I should've died, too. Wouldn't that have been perfect for you? You could've gone on fucking that bitch and—"

"Anjali," her husband silenced her with just her name. He didn't say it in anger or even loudly, he said it patiently, gracefully. "Why don't you sit down, and I'll see him out?"

"Why will you see him out? What is he to you?" she asked wildly. Her eyes were red, swollen, and her untidy hair flowed loosely and framed her face.

Anju's husband made her sit down, then he walked out with me into the open area beyond the doors of the intensive care unit lobby.

"I am really sorry," I began, and he waved his hands in dismissal.

"She is just distressed and . . . since she blames you, she got very upset," he said. "I am Sandeep Sharma." He held out his hand and I shook it like an automaton.

"Brigadier Prakash Mehra," I said. He knew who I was, but I didn't know what else to say.

"Why are you here, sir?"

He asked me with such frankness that I couldn't lie. "Because I feel responsible for your son's illness."

"No." He shook his head. "He is our son. You are not responsible in any way."

"But I did this to him, to all of you." It was not a man's place to cry, but it was not every day that I found out I was to blame for a little boy's impending death. "I forgot to pick her up and . . . One night and all our lives have changed forever."

Sandeep just stood there. "Please don't feel responsible. It was an accident."

"I never meant this to happen."

"You couldn't have known," he agreed.

I looked at my polished shoes and then at him. "I . . . can arrange for . . . I can try at least to move your son to the military hospital. They have better doctors and they have better services."

For a moment I wondered if I had insulted him.

"If you could manage that, we would be very grateful," he said humbly.

"I hope you don't mind."

"If it will make my son comfortable, sir, I will sell my soul."

I started to pull strings as soon as I reached my office. I called Colonel Puri, who commanded the military hospital, and asked if he could do anything. According to the rule book, Colonel Puri couldn't do anything, but he and I knew each other from before and he owed me a few favors.

He asked me the inevitable question: "Who are these people?"

A boy's life was at stake. I wasn't going to hide behind lies. "My ex-wife and her son."

Colonel Puri didn't ask any more questions, he just told me that he would send an army ambulance to pick up the boy from the government hospital. I would have to sign some papers and the boy's parents would have to do the same.

I went back to the government hospital. This time only Sandeep was sitting outside in the lobby. He rose as soon as he saw me.

"They will move him to the military hospital today," I told him without preamble. "And the doctor there will have a look at his medical files and see what can be done."

"Thank you very much," he said sincerely, and I felt like the smallest man ever born. I had been feeling smug outside his house a few hours ago, thinking Anju had to work because her new husband couldn't support his family on his own. Now, this man's love for his child and his dignity humbled me.

"How is he now?" I asked.

He shrugged.

"And Anju?"

"Anjali is better. I should go and tell her what you have done for us."

"I am not doing any favors," I said sincerely. For the first time in my life I was hiding behind nothing. I was bare, naked, and vulnerable. I hadn't known that truth could be this debilitating and this exhilarating.

All my dealings with Anju had been less than honest, tainted with some selfish need. This time was no different. However, for the first time, I was able to acknowledge the truth. I knew that to be able to stand seeing myself shave in the mirror every morning I had to make amends, I had to help Anju's son. It was a purely selfish act.

"I am trying to relieve my guilt," I confessed.

Sandeep smiled and patted my shoulder. "So many others wouldn't even have felt guilt."

❧ T W E N T Y - O N E

S A N D E E P

"Don't cut off your nose to spite your face, Anjali," I warned her. "Amar will be more comfortable and in a military hospital they will be able to give him better care."

"But I'll owe him, Sandeep," she said wretchedly.

"So we'll owe him," I said. "Does it matter so much?"

Amar was sedated, breathing through a tube. She looked at his lifeless form for several minutes.

"No, it doesn't matter at all," she said, defeated.

Then she clutched my shirt and wept soundlessly into my chest.

Amar was moved to the military hospital that evening. The hospital even sent an ambulance, and when I asked them how I should pay them, they said it had been taken care of. I wanted to object. I didn't want her ex-husband to take care of my son, but I didn't say anything. I would settle the matter later with Prakash. Whatever the price, I was prepared to pay it.

I had just told Anjali that pride didn't matter, but I did

feel pride. I felt the pinch of not being able to give my son the best medical care because I couldn't afford it. But this was not the time for guilt and pride. Our son's fragile life needed a miracle and I was happily prepared to subdue guilt and pride for it.

Major Mukesh Mohan, the resident pulmonologist, went through Amar's files carefully. He addressed Anjali as madam or Mrs. Sharma, and me as Sandeep. He seemed very proficient and sharp. I was relieved and prayed that he would be the miracle we were waiting for.

He lit a cigarette as soon as we all settled down in his office. His overflowing ashtray indicated he was a chain smoker. He had probably heard all the jokes there were about the smoking lung doctor who didn't take his own advice.

Major Mohan's office was not very large and the several file cabinets lining the walls made the office seem smaller than it was. The window shades were open and sunlight bloomed into the room exposing the untidy office.

"I have had a few cases from the Bhopal gas tragedy, but they were relatively minor. This is very advanced," he said. "Madam, I am very sorry that you got trapped there that night. I have heard some scary stories from colleagues who were posted in Bhopal then."

"I only got bronchial asthma, while Amar has . . . so many problems," Anjali said, tears rolling down her cheeks. She'd been crying since Amar had been hospitalized. I wondered if she would ever stop.

"Usually pulmonary fibrosis is seen in adults over the age of forty. In this case, because of the methyl isocyanate gas, his lungs have deteriorated. We still don't know how damaging the gas really was. New lung diseases caused by the gas seem to keep cropping up, and your son also had a heart valve problem, right?" He flipped through Amar's file.

"He had a valve stenosis," I said. "They operated and . . . it didn't improve his condition."

Major Mohan nodded and looked up from the file. "It is too late to do a lung or heart transplant. The length of the disease has made him very weak. Chances are he won't make it through surgery, so recovering from such complex surgery is out of the question.

"I will do some tests, but I don't think the diagnosis is going to be much different."

We both looked at him as if he were the supreme judge. We'd heard all of this before. From doctors in Hyderabad, doctors in Ooty, doctors in Bombay, and now we had hoped that this major would sing a different song.

"Most of his lungs have been eaten away by scar tissue, and his lower respiratory tract, according to these reports, has lost many functional alveolar units. That is why he is having trouble breathing." He looked up and sighed. "I am sorry, I should have explained. Alveolar units are—"

"We know," I interrupted him. "We did a lot of research when he was born and the doctors told us all about it. He couldn't breathe properly when he was born." I didn't know how I was speaking so calmly because I was feeling like Anjali was looking like a mass of tears and broken dreams.

"I can put him on a respirator for a while, but it is just a matter of time," Major Mohan said, just as the doctor at the government hospital had told us earlier. "We will make him as comfortable as we can and we will make sure he is not in pain."

"You will drug him?" I asked.

"Yes, probably morphine to ease the pain and we will make sure he breathes, but . . ."

"You are making him ready . . . ready to die," Anjali said, her lips folding as her eyes sparkled with a fresh batch of tears. "He was fine a week ago. He even walked a little."

"This has been going on since he was born. It is amazing he has lived for so long. He could walk a week ago because he had a good day, not because he was getting better," the doctor said sympathetically. "We will make sure he has his own room. We will put an extra bed there, so that one of you can stay with him at all times. A nurse will be on call twenty-four hours a day. We will . . . help in every way possible."

"You will help him die," Anjali said indignantly. "My son is going to die."

"I am so sorry, Mrs. Sharma. But he was born with—"

"He left me at the station," she said, slightly hysterical. "He said he forgot to pick me up. He left me there, while he slept."

I patted her hand and thanked the doctor.

"Do you know how unlucky I was?" she asked the doctor, who had stuffed his hands in his pockets. His face was drawn as if he could feel our pain, and I thought he could. He had done this before. He had given the news of a patient's impending death to hysterical and hopeful relatives.

"The wind was blowing in the other direction, away from the EME Center. The Union Carbide plant was just four kilometers away from where he was sleeping," she whimpered. "They were all saved, while I was left at the railway station."

She looked at me with sad eyes. Hope was dying. Our miracle was not here and she knew it, just as I did.

"There was a taxi driver, a Sardarji. He tried to get us out. He died on the steering wheel. Why didn't I die, too, Sandeep?"

I hugged her. My eyes were hazy with unshed tears.

"If I had died none of this would have happened. We wouldn't have to watch Amar die," she said, sobbing uncontrollably.

Major Mohan patted my shoulder. "You should get her to take some rest."

"I hate him, Sandeep," Anjali whispered. "I hate Prakash so much, I could kill him."

"Don't think about what happened, madam," the doctor said patiently. "Think about spending time with your child and making him comfortable and happy. He is going to be sedated a lot, but you can read to him and talk to him. He needs you right now."

She collapsed against me once more and I, too, hated Prakash at that moment.

My son was dying because of a simple accident. It could have happened to anyone and, to be perfectly fair, Prakash had not done it intentionally.

But it didn't matter. It didn't matter that he had gotten Amar into a good hospital and it didn't matter he was the reason Amar's last days would be comfortable. I hated him with an irrational bitterness. My son was dying and I didn't want to be fair or just anymore. Amar was twelve years old, he was my baby, my son. Where was the justice in his death?

↣ TWENTY-TWO

PRAKASH

I knocked on our bedroom door. According to the maid, Indu hadn't left our bedroom all day.

I had received a call from Major Mohan about Amar. My heart was heavy with guilt and grief and I needed Indu. She was my wife and even though we fought and were unhappy with each other about so many things, I needed her—after all, she was all I had.

I tried the doorknob and it turned.

She was sitting in an armchair staring out the window. She didn't even turn to look at me.

"Anju . . . Anjali has a twelve-year-old son," I told her. My voice was shaking and a cold storm was raging inside me. "He has a lung disease. He got the lung disease because I didn't pick her up that night at the railway station."

She turned to look at me without any emotions reflected in her voice or her face. "Is it your child?"

"No," I said, and kneeled down beside her. I took her

hands in mine. "I left her at the station, the night of the Bhopal gas tragedy. I forgot to pick her up. I didn't mean for it to happen." I didn't even know I was crying until I felt wet drops fall on our hands. "Now the boy has a lung problem because she spent the night in the city. Her son is going to die. Indu, I am a murderer."

I put my head down on her lap and cried like a child. I had never meant for any of it to happen—the marriage, her getting trapped in the railway station that night, or her son dying because of that night. It was a horrible mistake but I wasn't paying for it, Anju was. She and her son and her husband were paying for my negligence. I had to live with this forever and I didn't know how I could.

I felt my heart break when Indu pulled her hands away from mine. I wouldn't blame her if she wanted to leave me now. I would leave myself if I could.

With a generosity I did not deserve, Indu rested her hands on my head and stroked my hair.

"You didn't know," she said. "You didn't mean for her to be caught in the city that night."

"But it happened, anyway," I said, raising my eyes to see her.

She smiled. Her face held the calmness I had seen on Sandeep's face. "Life is like that, Prakash. You can't plan it."

"He is going to die and . . . I moved him to the military hospital," I told her. "That is the least I could do."

"That is all you can do," she corrected me. "I love you, Prakash."

"And I love you, Indu," I said, feeling a weight lift off my chest. "This will always be with us."

"You are not a murderer."

"She thinks I am."

"She is a mother," she said softly.

"I didn't do this on purpose, Indu, none of it. You believe me, don't you?"

"I believe you."

I put my head in her lap again, drawing on her warmth, her comfort, and her scent.

"I never cheated on you." My voice was gruff with tears and muffled against the silk of her sari.

"I know. I never cheated on you either."

"I never doubted you."

"We'll take Mamta and Mohit to the hospital and meet her son. What's his name?" she asked.

"Amar." A name given to someone who would live forever. Amar meant someone who could never die.

Her stoic calm eroded. She burst into tears then and we mourned a child that was not ours, but who still was a part of us. For twelve years of his life, neither of us knew Amar existed. Now we did and we wept for his short life and we wept because I was to blame.

❧ TWENTY-THREE

ANJALI

When I found out I was pregnant, I was deliriously happy. I had missed a period and went to the doctor immediately, hoping, wishing, and praying. Sandeep had a class he couldn't miss, so I went alone.

It took a couple of hours for the blood test results to come back, but I waited, pacing the clinic floors, walking in the garden outside.

I imagined how the doctor would tell me and then how I would tell Sandeep. I wanted a child so much. I wanted to be a mother. I wanted to give my child unconditional love. To give my child everything I didn't have and more.

I wanted to see Sandeep play with our baby, to hear him croon and talk baby talk. I wanted to see Sandeep carry our baby on his shoulder and teach him how to play cricket.

When the test results came back, an amazing thing happened. I forgot about the past and embraced my future. For the first time since my divorce I could look forward, and look for-

202

ward with no cynicism. A child was growing within me. It was a gift, the most beautiful gift I had ever been given, and I was so happy that I couldn't feel bad about the past anymore. I couldn't feel sorry for myself anymore for what I had gone through with Prakash. God had made up for it all by giving me this baby.

Sandeep was still in class when I knocked on the door of his classroom and grinned from ear to ear.

"Got to go," Sandeep told his class. "My wife's pregnant." The class cheered and Sandeep looked like he had been offered a piece of heaven.

We were still at the Hyderabad Central University then. I was teaching in the elementary school on campus and we had what one might call an idyllic life. We were happy and life was one big honeymoon, just like in the movies. And just like it often happens in the movies, the happiness was fleeting and the contentment ephemeral.

Pregnancy was wonderful. I enjoyed the feeling of life inside me, and I loved feeling the baby kick as he grew. It was a magical experience, to carry a child, a child that had a little bit of me, a little bit of Sandeep, and a whole lot of himself. We had made a person, a whole person, all by ourselves and I was giddy with joy.

Sarita had had her daughter a year ago and she was full of advice. Harjot came to stay with us the last fortnight of my pregnancy to help me through what was going to be, according to her, the most physically painful experience of my life. She was not a gynecologist so she couldn't deliver my baby, but she was all set to do everything else.

It was midnight when my labor began.

I woke Sandeep up. "I feel funny."

"Funny, ha, ha, or funny, peculiar?" he asked groggily, half asleep.

"Funny? I am going to have a baby!" I squealed when a contraction gripped me and he woke up.

Harjot, Gopi, and Sarita waited in the hospital lounge, while Sandeep fought with the entire nursing staff to get into the delivery room. Those days they didn't allow fathers in. The father waited outside with a box of sweets and distributed them as soon as a nurse walked out and told him that the mess was cleaned up and that the baby was a boy or a girl.

Sandeep wouldn't be deterred. "That is my child," he explained to the nursing staff in a calm voice. "I am going to be there." After that no one could budge him, and I don't think the nurses really wanted to invite security to remove him from his wife's bedside.

Sandeep had bruises on his hand when it was all over. Small scrapes, scratches, marks from my fingers were evidence of my labor. But he didn't notice them and I soon forgot all about my tedious fifteen-hour labor. We were worried about our baby because they had rushed Amar away even before I could see him.

"Is something wrong?" I asked Sandeep, because Harjot had told me that they would lay my baby on my stomach and let him breastfeed immediately.

"He was not getting enough oxygen," the doctor told us when he came back to our hospital room. "We have put him in an incubator. Maybe there is a problem with his lungs."

Thus began a nightmare that never really ended. We went

from specialist to specialist and were finally told that Amar's breathing problems were related to the methyl isocyanate gas I had inhaled in the Bhopal Railway Station.

But that was years ago and I couldn't understand how something that happened so long ago could affect my baby. Then I found out more about the deadly gas and how I shouldn't have more children, that any child we had would probably have the same set of problems. Some of the specialists said that they were surprised that I had even gotten pregnant. One of the symptoms of inhaling methyl isocyanate gas was infertility.

And just like that, my past took over my future.

"Mummy?" Amar stirred.

"I am here."

He opened his eyes and looked around. The room was unfamiliar. He didn't know he had been moved to the military hospital.

"We moved you to a better hospital," Sandeep said. He was standing on the other side of the bed.

Amar assessed his condition by looking at the tubes that were inserted in him, one inside his nose and one IV tube coming out of his hand.

I bit back the tears. "Just to help you breathe," I explained.

He took a deep breath and then frowned through the tubes. "I can't breathe on my own?"

"Just for a little while," Sandeep said.

"I am thirsty."

We were instructed not to give him anything to eat or drink while he was being fed intravenously.

"How about some ice chips?" I suggested, and opened the small icebox next to his bed. I wet his lips and his mouth and let the ice chip fall on my hand when he spat it out. I wiped my hands on my sari and waited to see if he wanted more ice.

He knew. I could see it in his eyes.

The knowledge of death was a very big responsibility to shove on such a young boy. Adults who had lived a full life were afraid of death; a twelve-year-old boy must be petrified and outraged at the injustice. He had barely lived and now he had to face death. He had seen and done so little, had so many dreams and aspirations, none of which would come to fruition.

He should die easily, without knowing he is going to die, I prayed.

Sometimes I used to dream that a pill would be invented that would completely cure Amar. I used to wish for a miracle, but now I knew there were no miracles. His lungs were beyond repair and his heart was slowing down. Major Mohan had told us that it was only a matter of time, that respiratory failure was imminent.

Sandeep, Komal, and I took shifts by Amar's bed. Although she hated me, Komal loved my son, and she sat with him, reading from storybooks and giving him ice chips whenever he woke up.

Gopi and Sarita insisted on staying with Amar so that Sandeep and I could get some rest. But I was there even when they came by.

Sandeep phoned and told my parents that Amar was very

sick. They asked if we wanted them to come, but Sandeep asked them not to. The train journey was over ten hours and we had enough problems without dealing with my parents' aggravating presence.

I couldn't leave Amar's side. I stood guard as if I could fight against destiny, against death.

"He might still get well," Komal tried to console me. "He talked last night."

He had talked for about two minutes before falling back to sleep. I had never felt this helpless before. I had always fought against fate and what life offered me, and I had tried to win each time. This time there was nothing I could do but let him die. But I was his mother. Wasn't it my job to save him and protect him? He was in this world, in this hospital, because I had birthed him.

I couldn't blame Prakash anymore with a clear conscience. He had given Amar a better hospital and better medical care. I would forever be grateful. This Prakash was different from the selfish Prakash I knew. This Prakash felt pain and guilt. I wished him the best in his life. Sandeep was right, it didn't matter that we owed him.

Promises meant nothing if breaking them could help our son.

After Prakash had said he wouldn't give me any alimony, I had vowed to never take anything from him. I had promised myself that I'd never let him into my life again. I had promised myself that I'd never speak to him again. And I was doing all those things and feeling no regret. How could I have any ego, any shame where Amar was concerned?

Sandeep came to the hospital in the evening and sat with

Amar. One of us still had to work. We had not managed to save any money since Amar was born and our lives still had to go on somehow even if our son's wouldn't.

Sandeep read him stories, about fairies and goblins and pixies. He brought Amar's record player to the hospital and we played Kishore Kumar's comedic Hindi movie songs alternated with his serious ones. I read him Shakespeare.

It had been just four days since he had been admitted to the hospital, but it felt like a lifetime. As if we had been there forever and Amar's hospital room was our home.

The nurses were warm and kind and they even fed Sandeep and me. They checked on me when they checked on Amar. I was treated like a brigadier's wife.

On the fifth day of our bedside vigil, in the evening before Sandeep came, two children peeped into the room. They introduced themselves very nicely: Mamta and Mohit Mehra.

Prakash's wife followed them. Prakash hadn't come to check on Amar, though I had a feeling he was in constant touch with Major Mohan.

Indu stood beside Amar and smiled at me tentatively, while her children scrambled toward the area where I had piled up storybooks and comics.

"How is he today?" she whispered.

"The same," I said.

"Prakash said they will take him off the respirator so that he can breathe on his own," she said.

"Tomorrow."

She had tears in her eyes and I wanted to tell her not to cry for my son.

"Please thank Prakash for what he did." It had to be said. "We will forever be—"

"He didn't do it to be thanked," she said sternly. "He did it so that he could sleep at night."

"Whatever his reasons—"

"Please," she implored. "Don't thank him. He is torn by what's happened. He doesn't know how to make amends and this is the only thing he could think of."

Amar stirred a little, and I waited for him to open his eyes, but he didn't. He went back to sleep.

"He sleeps most of the day. He wakes up once in a while . . ." I explained, my voice breaking.

"Mamta, leave that alone." Indu rushed to her daughter, who was trying rip a page out of a comic book.

I smiled. Children did things like that. Children who had strength and who were healthy. Amar had done some of the naughty things children did, but he was usually too tired to do much. He had been active when he was two and then all of a sudden his health had deteriorated. It was like living on the edge of a sword; a small slip could result in a fatal wound.

Indu and her children stayed a little longer and then left.

When Sandeep arrived in the evening, I told him about their visit and he only nodded wearily. The long hours of the day and night were taking their toll on him, but like me he couldn't sleep, even if he wanted to.

"I called Harjot," Sandeep said. "She is coming the day after tomorrow."

"You shouldn't have asked her to come. She has a family and—"

"I don't think I could stop her," Sandeep said. "I had to tell her about Amar and then she said she would be here."

"How long will she stay?"

"She said as long as we need her."

Major Mohan came by three times a day and kept insisting that I was going to fall sick if I didn't sleep a little and eat properly.

But how could I eat or sleep when I was waiting for something to happen? Something I didn't want.

The next day Major Mohan took the respirator off and we waited again, holding our breath. Amar struggled a few times and then started to breathe erratically.

"We will see how this works for eight hours," Major Mohan said.

I was tempted to ask, What happens after eight hours? Do they leave him to die, or do they put him back on the respirator? A part of me wanted him to live by any means possible, yet another part knew Amar would hate being bound to a machine.

Prakash came the night Amar was taken off the respirator. He looked haggard, old, and tired. He had aged in a matter of days.

He stood by the door of Amar's room and talked to Sandeep for a while. I wondered irritably when those two had become such good friends.

Prakash came inside the room and stood by Amar's bed. He looked down at me as I sat on a chair on the other side of the bed holding Amar's hand.

"I spoke to Major Mohan," he told me. "Can I do anything else?"

I wanted to yell at him, but a man had to be given a second chance—even a man like Prakash.

"You have done more than I could have asked for," I said sincerely. "I want to thank you, but your wife said I shouldn't."

I was never going to really forgive Prakash for leaving me in that railway station that night or for ruining our marriage, but I would try. Prakash, my ex-husband, had made the mistakes; Prakash, the man who stood by my son's side, was trying his best to make amends.

"That was a nice thing to say to Prakash," Sandeep told me, when we kept vigil into the wee hours of the night. The nurse kept coming in to check Amar's vital signs, keeping us awake.

I could hear every breath he took because of the grating sound he made. But Major Mohan had assured us that Amar was in no pain and, for now, that was enough.

"That was a very nice thing he did for Amar," I said.

Sandeep put his arm around me and rocked me slowly. We were sitting together in a large cane chair as we had every night, waiting for the inevitable, hoping for a miracle.

How would we live after Amar? Would we ever be happy again? Would we always be sad?

"It will all work out," Sandeep said as if he could read my thoughts. "As long as you and I and god are together, we can do anything."

"Except save our son."

"God isn't with us on this one," he said.

That night we fell asleep against each other, our dreams and nightmares colliding.

❧ TWENTY-FOUR

ANJALI

Sandeep woke me up at five in the morning. Harjot's train arrived at six and he had to go to the railway station.

He kissed Amar on the forehead and looked at him for a long time. I knew each time he went away he was afraid that when he came back, Amar would be gone.

I was afraid, too, because I couldn't imagine how I would tell him that our son was no more.

He kissed me on the mouth and told me to go back to sleep, even though he knew I wouldn't.

After Sandeep left, I opened a book of Yeats and started to recite Amar's favorite poem. He loved "The Second Coming." I had asked him if he even knew what it meant.

"No," he had said honestly. "But I like the words and I like it when you say '*Spiritus Mundi.*'"

Amar's eyes flickered open when I reached the *Spiritus Mundi* part, and I smiled.

"I like that part," he whispered.

He opened his eyes wide and I thought, Maybe I should call the nurse so that she can give him more morphine.

"Are you in pain? Do you want more painkillers?"

He shook his head. "Too many tubes, Mummy."

"I know, *beta,* but it will—"

"Can you take them off?"

I didn't know what to do. I stood up and looked around helplessly. I wanted to argue with him, but how could I?

"I want to go outside, Mummy."

I wanted to cry out, "Wait, wait, my son, please wait. Just a minute more, an hour more, a lifetime more."

"Outside, *beta?*" I managed to say through the constriction in my throat.

"I want some fresh air."

I didn't hesitate. I carefully removed the IV needle from the back of his hand and separated the electrodes, which were counting the beats of his heart, from his chest. The machine made the insidious beeping that implied death. I ignored it and carried him. He was so frail, like he had been when he was a baby.

I put him on the wheelchair, wiping my tears away because I didn't want him to see me crying.

I wheeled him through a small corridor and opened the door to a balcony. It was a cold morning so I put my shawl around him.

"It is nice here," he said, but his voice was weak.

I sat down on a chair next to him and held his hand.

He struggled to breathe, once, twice, three, four times, and then he stopped struggling.

I held his limp hand in mine without looking at his face. I couldn't see the rolling hills, the trees, or the garden glittering in the beauty of dawn. It was blinding, this moment. This un-recoverable, inescapable moment.

I sat there for a long time holding my son's hand.

I stared into oblivion, my mind blank. No thought, no emotion surfaced as I sat numbly in the cold holding my baby's hand.

"Madam." A nurse's voice jolted me out of my present emptiness and launched me into yet another.

"Madam?" she asked with concern.

I smiled through the pain. "He wanted a breath of fresh air," I said.